S0-ARL-937

Luc's jaw clenched. "I don't run away from anything."
Or anyone, he thought.

Celeste didn't look convinced. "Don't worry, *Mr.* Dante. You don't have to run from me if we happen to see each other on the street."

"We're on opposite sides," Luc muttered.

"Opposite sex, yes. Opposite sides, I don't think so. We have the same goals. We both want to see the good guy win." And with that, she moved away.

Luc could swear Celeste Bradshaw had just gotten the best of him. He left the bar before he could give in to the suggestions racing through his mind. Foremost would have been to drag her over the bar and kiss her senseless.

Maybe if he gave in to his baser instincts, he'd be able to get her out of his system—before insanity took over.

Dear Reader,

The days are hot and the reading is hotter here at Silhouette Intimate Moments. Linda Turner is back with the next of THOSE MARRYING McBRIDES! in *Always a McBride.* Taylor Bishop has only just found out about his familial connection—and he has no idea it's going to lead him straight to love.

In *Shooting Starr,* Kathleen Creighton ratchets up both the suspense and the romance in a story of torn loyalties you'll long remember. Carla Cassidy returns to CHEROKEE CORNERS in *Last Seen...,* a novel about two people whose circumstances ought to prevent them from falling in love but don't. *On Dean's Watch* is the latest from reader favorite Linda Winstead Jones, and it will keep you turning the pages as her federal marshal hero falls hard for the woman he's supposed to be keeping an undercover watch over. *Roses After Midnight,* by Linda Randall Wisdom, is a suspenseful look at the hunt for a serial rapist—and the blossoming of an unexpected romance. Finally, take a look at Debra Cowan's *Burning Love* and watch passion flare to life between a female arson investigator and the handsome cop who may be her prime suspect.

Enjoy them all—and come back next month for more of the best and most exciting romance reading around.

Yours,

Leslie J. Wainger
Executive Editor

Please address questions and book requests to:
Silhouette Reader Service
U.S.: 3010 Walden Ave., P.O. Box 1325, Buffalo, NY 14269
Canadian: P.O. Box 609, Fort Erie, Ont. L2A 5X3

Roses After Midnight

LINDA RANDALL WISDOM

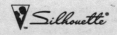

INTIMATE MOMENTS™

Published by Silhouette Books

America's Publisher of Contemporary Romance

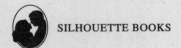

SILHOUETTE BOOKS

ISBN 0-373-27305-3

ROSES AFTER MIDNIGHT

Copyright © 2003 by Words by Wisdom

This edition published by arrangement with Harlequin Books S.A.

® and TM are trademarks of Harlequin Books S.A., used under license.
Trademarks indicated with ® are registered in the United States Patent
and Trademark Office, the Canadian Trade Marks Office and in other
countries.

Visit Silhouette at www.eHarlequin.com

Printed in U.S.A.

LINDA RANDALL WISDOM

grew up never imagining being anything other than a writer. In high school, her journalism instructor encouraged her fiction writing, but in college, her journalism adviser told her she wouldn't get anywhere in fiction writing, while women were needed in the newspaper field. She wasn't totally derailed, just delayed for a while until the day she wrote her first two novels, *Dancer in the Shadows* and *Fourteen Karat Beauty,* which she sold to Silhouette Romance on her wedding anniversary in 1979. From that day on, she never looked back.

She lives in Southern California with her husband, a spoiled-rotten terrier/Chihuahua mix named Bogie, who's also on her Web site, four parrots, five Siamese fighting fish and a tortoise named Florence. All of her pets have shown up in her books. She also likes to include at least one true incident in each book. Many of them have come from friends and prove that truth is stranger than fiction!

She can be contacted through her Web site http://occrwa.com/lindawisdom.

Many thanks to my agent, Karen Solem, for being there when I needed her and for reminding me I can do it.

Prologue

Nancy couldn't stop smiling. For once, Gary had actually listened to her!

Earlier that evening, she'd come home, once again furious with her boyfriend for caring more about spending time at a sports bar called The End Zone watching football than spending time with her. Even after she'd warned him at lunch the other day that she was sick and tired of his wanting to be with his friends more than he wanted to be with her. How could he tell her she was important to him, then go off with his idiot friends?

She'd come back to their apartment with her mind firmly made up. As far as she was concerned, the man was out of second chances.

She wasn't sure what later woke her out of her light sleep. She'd been about to scream when a hand gently covered her mouth.

"Let me show you how I really feel about you," a man had whispered against her ear.

Then he had backed up his words with deeds. And such wonderful deeds they were.

To keep with the mystery, he'd covered her eyes with a silk scarf, insisted on the lights remaining off, kept his voice at a whisper and, afterwards, had drawn her a bath and even washed her hair before carrying her back to bed. Afterwards, he'd left as silently as he arrived. She couldn't understand why he insisted on the mystery, but she wasn't about to complain as long as he was finally concentrating on her!

Now she lay there feeling exhilarated from the incredible night Gary had given her.

Her smile widened when she heard the door open and close.

Gary's back, she thought to herself as she sat up and switched on the lamp by the bed. She even thought about returning the favor.

Bumps against a wall heralded Gary's arrival before he finally lurched his way into the bedroom. The yeasty smell of beer surrounded him.

His face was slack and eyes glassy from too much alcohol.

"I'm sorry, baby, I'll make it up to you, I promise," he slurred. Unable to hold his balance, he fell onto the bed in a drunken heap and promptly passed out.

Chapter 1

"Do you care to tell me what Luc Dante has to do with Prince Charming, Bradshaw?"

The growled demand was enough to make anyone quaver with fear. Chief of Detectives Sam Adams was an imposing man. A former marine with a bite to match his bark, he was known to take no prisoners and suffer no idiots. And that was if he was in a good mood.

Oddly, Detective Celeste Bradshaw never felt any fear of the man. But she still did her best to never cross him.

Right now, she was working on perhaps two hours sleep, five cups of coffee that had turned to acid in her stomach and a cinnamon muffin that she'd eaten hours ago. In other words, her nerves were humming.

"Lieutenant, Parker and I have come up with a common thread we've recently discovered in the Prince Charming case."

The man considered her with a decided lack of expression. She didn't think she'd ever seen him smile. Rumor in the station was that if the man smiled, you knew you were in deep trouble.

"So you're saying Luc Dante is that thread?" he asked. "You do realize you're talking about the man whose restaurant held a private dinner for the mayor and the city council last night when the last rape occurred?"

Celeste lowered her voice. "Yes, sir, I do. But one thing the victims had in common was the fact they had all dined at Dante's Cafe."

"A lot of people eat there. Hell, I do," he pointed out. "Are you saying you think Dante is Prince Charming?" he said between clenched teeth, glowering at her.

She kept her courage before her like a shield as she faced him. "No, sir, we don't think he's the rapist. But we do feel there could be a connection between the restaurant and the rapes."

Sam still regarded her with a stern gaze. "And Parker agrees with all this?"

"I agree with Bradshaw," Dylan Parker said, walking up to them. "When last night's victim recounted her schedule for the past few days, she mentioned she and her boyfriend having lunch at Dante's Cafe a couple days ago. We called Mr. Dante this morning and asked him if he'd come by the station."

"When you don't consider a man a suspect, you don't have him come to the station for any kind of questioning." The lieutenant did not look happy.

"There's more involved than just that," Celeste replied. "We're hoping he'll be willing to help us."

The lieutenant cocked his head as he listened to her plan. He finally nodded. "If you screw up, it will all be on your head." With that, he walked off.

Dylan shook his head. "Well, that was heartwarming," he muttered. "Nothing like getting that warm and fuzzy feeling from your boss." He glanced at his partner. "Ready to play cop?" He gestured to the closed door to their right.

She nodded as she picked up her notes. "Let's do it."

Celeste opened the door and stopped short.

Ohmigod!

Luc didn't like feeling closed in.

When he received a phone call that morning from a Detective Celeste Bradshaw asking him to come down to the police station, he had been tempted to turn her request over to his attorney. He knew he hadn't done anything remotely illegal in the past seventeen years, so there was no reason for him to be here. Hell, he even overfed the parking meters. But she'd said she hoped he could help them with a case. Luc never gave in to curiosity, but there was something about the lady's voice that had him wondering what the face looked like. Recalling the cops he'd dealt with twenty-some years ago, he figured she would look like someone's nightmare.

At the station, an officer had ushered him into an interview room and closed the door. As Luc sat waiting for the detective to come in, he felt a strangling sensation as if all the air had been sucked out of the small room. To get his mind off the feeling, he looked around.

Some things never change. No pictures on walls that were painted what he would call "institutional green." The only furniture was a plain wooden table and three equally plain chairs that were as uncomfortable as hell. But then, who wants prisoners comfortable during their interrogation? At least this room didn't have a mirror, so he wouldn't wonder who was observing him from the other side.

Why the hell was he here?

He turned his head when the door opened. A woman and man entered.

She definitely wasn't his idea of a cop.

"Mr. Dante, I'm Detective Bradshaw and this is my partner, Detective Parker." The woman smiled at him as she held out her hand. "Would you care for something to drink? Some coffee, perhaps?"

"I'd prefer being told why I'm here," Luc said, taking her hand even though a part of him didn't want to. *Forget what they told you as a kid. Cops aren't your friends.*

"Actually, Mr. Dante, we're hoping you can help us out." Detective Parker's smile didn't have the twenty-four-karat quality of Detective Bradshaw's. His was more "we're just buddies here."

Bull.

Luc kept his attention on Bradshaw. Cops had sure changed since he dealt with them on a regular basis. She not only dressed better, she smelled better. If he wasn't mistaken, the tailored shirt she wore was silk, and he'd hazard a guess that one ounce of her perfume cost more than most police detectives make in a month. Delicately etched features, shoulder-length golden-blond hair pulled back and secured at the nape with a black ribbon, large eyes that were an intriguing blend of green and gray, a generous mouth colored a light rose, and discreet gold hoop earrings.

She was easily the most beautiful woman he'd ever seen and he damned his mind and body for reacting to her.

Luc wondered how her partner dealt with working with someone so lovely. He was another one to watch out for. The man had a face too young for the gray hair, and his equally gray eyes were the kind that saw too much. Luc figured out their intentions right away. He played bad cop to the lady's good cop.

"Mr. Dante, we have asked you to come down in hopes that you can help us," Celeste said, taking the chair across from him.

Luc noticed Parker turned his chair around and sat down, resting his arms along the back. He guessed that the couple was not a "couple." While there was a sense of their being in tune with each other, there was no sense of their sharing more than a job.

"Planning a special dinner for the Chief of Police?" Luc asked, a sarcastic edge to his voice. Dammit, he didn't want to be here!

She ignored his tone. "We'd like to take you into our confidence and hope you'll understand why you can't discuss anything we tell you," she went on. "I'm sure you've read the stories about a serial rapist we've had in the area who's been called Prince Charming."

Luc jumped to his feet. He slammed his palms down on the tabletop, which rocked under the force. "What the hell is going on that you call me in here about the rapist?"

Neither moved.

"First off, Mr. Dante, you are not considered a suspect. But what we've discovered in our investigation is that every one of Prince Charming's victims has been a regular visitor to your restaurant," Celeste said. "As I said, we do not believe you personally have anything to do with the rapes, but we do feel Dante's Cafe could be a link."

Luc felt a pressure in his chest that threatened to cut off his airway. He'd sweated blood to build his dream. He'd done this to give himself a second chance and offer the same to others. And now the police were telling him that there was a good chance someone he knew was behind a series of rapes. He didn't give a damn what kind of spin they were trying to put on the situation, he knew the score.

The lady was telling him that while he wasn't considered a suspect, someone working at his restaurant could very well be. This wasn't the kind of publicity any business owner needed.

He may as well close the doors now.

"Your reasoning for the restaurant being a link is that the victims dined there," he said. "There's been— what?—four, five rapes in the past six months, correct? A great deal more than four or five women have eaten there in the past week alone." He speared Bradshaw with a chilling gaze.

It didn't even faze her. She leafed through her notebook but didn't look down to consult her notes as she spoke.

"Two days ago Nancy Gerard and Gary Young celebrated Nancy's birthday at Dante's Cafe," she said. "Last night, someone broke in to her apartment and raped her. Janice Bowen had lunch there about once a week since it was near her office. Barbara Miller was another frequent customer, along with Lauren Davis and Marie Richardson. We think there could be even more victims who haven't reported the crime for one reason or another. Unfortunately, many rape victims don't come forward."

"Which is not good publicity for the town, is it." Luc wondered how someone who looked like her was willing to be a cop. "The town council knows the tourist trade will dry up if the rapist continues attacking. No one cares if he's called Prince Charming."

"I'm glad to hear you say that," she said, ignoring the bite to his words. "We'd like to place someone undercover in your restaurant."

Luc's first reaction was to laugh. His second was to tell her "no way in hell!" He chose laughter.

"Really? What if I refuse your kind offer? What will you do next? Will the Health Department show up with a variety of infractions or the Fire Department cite me for new fire violations?"

"None of the above. We just want someone in there to observe. As it happens, you need a bartender and I have bartending experience."

"What?" Luc heard her partner's snort of disbelief echo his own. Aha. The lady hadn't discussed that idea with Parker.

"That's not what we discussed," Parker muttered.

She ignored him, too, as she leaned across the table. "I worked six nights a week as a bartender when I was in college. You name a drink, I can make it," she said confidently.

"If anyone goes in there undercover, it should be me," Parker told her.

Bradshaw shook her head. "The only drink you can whip up is a mean margarita." She turned back to Luc. "To begin the charade, l will even come in to properly interview for the job."

"Tell me something, Detective Bradshaw. Have you ever worked undercover before?" Luc asked, when what he really wanted to say was that the last thing he wanted was a cop working in his restaurant.

She smiled. "Yes, I have. Look, Mr. Dante, I'm

afraid of the rapist striking again and I'll do whatever it takes to get to him first," she replied.

"Understandable, but how do you know a friend won't come into the restaurant and blow your cover?"

"It's a common fact that few people truly look at anyone who serves them. A proper server is usually considered nothing more than a piece of furniture."

His glance skated over her. "I can't imagine anyone seeing you as a piece of furniture."

Parker shrugged. "Personally, I always thought she looked like one of those fancy side tables," he murmured, deadpan.

Luc looked from one to the other. The set expressions on their faces told him they weren't going to give up. They were determined to solve their case, and if they had to drag him into it, they would.

He'd fought long and hard for the life he had now. It appeared that if he didn't want any trouble with the police he'd have to go along with their plan.

If nothing else, he could prove no one at the cafe had anything to do with the rapes.

Luc stood up and turned to Bradshaw.

"If that's the case, be at the restaurant at ten a.m.," he instructed. "And be prepared to work tomorrow night's shift. My people aren't dumb, Detective. There's an excellent chance they'll make you for a cop the minute you step in the door."

"Then, I'll just have to make sure they don't, won't I," she said quietly. "Also, we'd appreciate you not telling anyone else the truth about me."

His dark-as-night eyes flared fire bright. "My partners need to know what's going on."

Dylan spoke up. "No, sir, they don't. We only told you because you're the most visible figure there. That's why we're asking you to cooperate with us. If we'd wanted to keep you in the dark, we would not have contacted you at all. Detective Bradshaw could have just walked in the door and applied for the job.''

Luc exhaled a deep breath. "With a good chance of not getting hired."

Dylan's expression was one only another male would understand.

"I think she would have."

Luc kept his gaze focused on Parker. He glanced briefly at Bradshaw.

"Then I will see you at ten."

Luc tapped his fingers briefly on the tabletop, then strode out of the room. The door closed behind him.

"I don't know about you, but I can see the man was clearly intimidated," Dylan commented with a slight twist of the lips as he and Celeste later exited the room and headed for their desks.

Celeste didn't reply. She sat down and checked phone messages that had been left there. She didn't see anything that needed an immediate response and pushed them to one side.

"He seemed to buy that I didn't know about your idea to work undercover," Dylan went on, even as he sensed his partner wasn't listening to him. He dropped into his chair and leaned back.

Celeste and Dylan enjoyed having a corner of the large room to themselves. They'd pushed their desks to face each other because they felt they communicated better that way.

She tossed her notebook on her desk. She had a hunch this wasn't going to be an easy assignment.

She'd looked into eyes that were so deep a blue they

appeared black. But she couldn't recall ever looking into eyes as empty as his. Many times before, she'd looked into eyes that were devoid of soul, of conscience. While Luc Dante's eyes weren't soulless, they were empty of all emotion.

What could happen to a man to bring about such rigid self-control?

She hadn't had much time to research Dante, so all she knew was that Luc Dante was thirty-five years old and single. He and two friends jointly owned the popular Dante's Cafe. A majority of the employees were people most businesses would refuse to hire because of their past police records. The three owners gave these people a much-needed fresh start, and so far few had abused their trust.

Celeste knew Luc Dante had grown up in a series of foster homes and had been a resident of the state more than once. But since his juvenile record was sealed, she wasn't able to find out more than what little she discovered during her hurried investigation.

None of her investigation warned her about the man himself. She'd had no idea his face looked like something etched on an ancient coin. Hair black as midnight curved over his collar. A slight olive cast to his skin spoke of a Mediterranean heritage. A fanciful part of her nature said a pirate must have stolen into his lineage. And those compelling eyes, framed by thick black lashes she couldn't achieve no matter how many coats of mascara she applied. Tall, whipcord lean, he looked as dangerous as a hungry panther, civilly dressed in a black fisherman's knit sweater, black jeans and black boots.

From the moment she stepped into the interrogation

room she felt the sheer raw male presence of the man as if he were the one in charge.

She looked across her desk at Dylan.

"We both agreed this was the way to do it," she said quietly.

Dylan nodded. He reached into a desk drawer and pulled out a bright pink spongy ball. He tossed it from one hand to the other, then to Celeste who caught it neatly with one hand.

"Nancy thought boyfriend Gary was surprising her with a night of some hot sex and a little danger," she said, throwing the ball back to Dylan.

"She wakes up, he's whispering to her he wants to give her love as he blindfolds her." The ball arced back to her.

"After he makes love to her, he fixes a bubble bath for her and even washes and dries her hair." She returns the ball to him. "He even cleans up the bathroom after he's finished."

"He doesn't take the blindfold off before he leaves, and when she pulls it off, she finds a red rose lying on the other pillow," Dylan continues the story as he tosses the ball back to her.

"She's in heaven. Gary's turned into this romantic guy instead of the jerk he's been lately."

Dylan reaches up and captures the ball again. "Until an hour later when ole Gary comes in drunk as the proverbial skunk and definitely not the Romeo Nancy frolicked with earlier. Gary sobers up fast, and Nancy's at the ER twenty minutes later."

Celeste nodded, recalling the phone call that got her out of bed at three a.m. More than eight hours later she was ready for a nap that she knew she wasn't going to get.

She rolled the ball between her palms as she glanced at the report on her desk. She wasn't reading anything she hadn't read before on this rapist.

"There was penetration, but no tearing of skin. No bruising along the inner thighs. In fact, the doctor didn't find bruises anywhere. There was a lack of semen, so the rapist must have used a condom and taken it with him, since it wasn't found anywhere in the apartment. The rape kit didn't give us anything new. Crime scene investigators didn't come up with any trace evidence in the rooms. Nothing was stolen from the apartment, even though Nancy's purse was out in plain sight, and she had about eighty dollars in cash in her wallet."

"She lost nothing but her trust," Dylan murmured. "Damn, Leste, this guy is running circles around us."

"Then, let's hope we can stop him before we all get dizzy." She closed her eyes momentarily, then opened them before she succumbed to the desperate need for sleep. A shadow crossed her and her desk rocked with faint movement. She looked to her right at the intruder.

The man sitting with one hip perched on the edge of her desk looked more like a criminal than a cop. He also didn't look very happy.

"I heard you hauled Luc Dante in." He shook his head in faint disgust. "Come on, Goldilocks, there is no way he's Prince Charming."

"We *asked* him to come in," she replied. "So tell me, Stryker, why are you interested in our activities? Domestic Crimes isn't your area of expertise."

He nodded. "True. I see dead people," he whispered dramatically.

"I hear they have medication for that now," Celeste said without missing a beat.

Jared Stryker leaned down until his lips almost

touched her ear. "Take it from me, Goldilocks, Luc Dante isn't the man you're looking for." He straightened up and ambled off, his stride fluid.

Celeste hated herself for watching him walk away. But the view of the man's rock-hard butt in faded jeans was way too good to waste, even if he could be a total jerk at times.

"Wipe the drool off your chin, Goldie," Dylan said, using Stryker's favorite nickname for her.

She knew she didn't look the least bit embarrassed at getting caught ogling a man.

"I've heard more than one woman say that Jared Stryker gives the term *strip search* an entirely new meaning," she told Dylan.

"That's more than I ever wanted to know." Dylan heaved a sigh. "Damn, Leste, thanks to that image I'm going to have to disinfect my mind's eye."

"That makes us even for your description of Winnie Jacobs." Celeste picked up her phone. "I guess I better see if I can pick up a different place to live and do a little work on changing myself into an ex-con looking for a job."

"Do you really think you'll learn something working undercover at the restaurant?" Dylan asked. "We could be wrong, you know. Maybe it is nothing more than a coincidence."

"And if we don't follow this and later learn it wasn't just a coincidence, we won't have to kick ourselves, Adams will do it for us. Right now, it's the only thing we've got, Dylan," Celeste replied. "If we don't find something soon, another woman is going to get raped." She leaned across her desk so no one could overhear her. "Last night, Nancy Gerard told me it was bad enough she'd been raped, but what upset her more was that she'd had an orgasm during the act. She saw it as the ultimate betrayal on her part. She can't believe she enjoyed it and that she had no idea it wasn't Gary Young."

"She shouldn't beat herself up over it. She honestly thought she was making love with her boyfriend," Dylan said.

Celeste nodded. "It's still very emotional, very traumatic. And something she isn't going to get over easily."

Dylan sighed. "In her shoes, I would hope I'd realize that I was still the victim."

"I'm hoping she'll realize that, too. A rape counselor had arrived to see her when I was leaving." She pulled out her PDA. "I've got some work ahead of me to get some things in place by tomorrow before my job interview."

He grinned. "I wouldn't worry. My sources tell me you're a shoo-in for the job."

Luc always breathed easier once he stepped inside Dante's Cafe.

It had nothing to do with the light and airy surroundings that belied the cold dark weather outside. Or the fact the restaurant was doing so well financially. Or even that one-third of it was all his.

It was because here he felt a sense of belonging. The people working here were like him. They were all misfits who hadn't been able to fit their square pegs in the round holes. People who had gotten off to a bad start and could have ended up in prison for life, or dead, if they hadn't been willing to do whatever it took to turn their lives around.

After the time he had spent yesterday at Sierra Vista's police department he craved all this even more.

Already he wasn't looking forward to a pretend interview that would result in a cop tending bar. He wondered how long it would take for someone here to catch on to Celeste Bradshaw's real purpose.

Luc stepped into the alcove where patrons waited to be seated. Sage-green velvet cushioned benches lined two walls, where leafy green plants stood in elegant vases. Luc stopped to finger one leaf that didn't look as green as the others. He'd have to ask Carl if the plant should be replaced. He liked everything to be perfect.

"Hey, boss man." A sprightly brunette woman appeared under the curved archway leading into the main dining room. "You're here early."

"I'm interviewing a new bartender this morning," he replied.

She opened the reservations book and wrote something down.

Luc studied the hostess with an objective eye. Gina wore an off-white tailored blouse with a knee-length black skirt. Evenings, the hostess would wear a calf-length skirt, and a dark red silk corsage would add color. Gina's heavy mass of black curly hair was pulled up into a knot at the back of her head. A black velvet ribbon with a small cameo graced her slender throat.

He doubted anyone would guess that four years ago Gina had been an integral part of a medical insurance fraud. She'd been an expert slip-and-fall artist who pretended to have accidents in stores or in front of unsuspecting motorists. She'd made a nice living out of it—until she made the mistake of trying her act on a judge's wife. Due to the large amount of money she'd milked from insurance companies, she went to jail for eighteen months. When she was released, she knew she didn't want to chance losing her three-year-old daughter. It hadn't been easy for her to find a job—until she applied at Dante's Cafe. She started out as a waitress, and when a former hostess left, she was offered the promotion.

Luc cocked his head at the sound of pots banging, wincing at the cacophony. He was relieved the restaurant wasn't open yet.

"Jimmy's trying out a new recipe," Gina explained. She rolled her eyes. "It's not going well."

He chuckled at the sound of curses rolling out of the kitchen. "So I hear. Paulie here, too?"

"In the office, where else. Are you sure he doesn't sleep there?"

"There have been times." Luc turned around when the front door opened and a woman stepped inside the foyer. He opened his mouth to explain Dante's was closed, then realized there was no need.

She offered him a brief impersonal smile as she passed him to approach Gina.

"May I help you?" Gina asked.

"Yes, I'm Celeste Bradley," she said in a low voice. "I have an appointment with Mr. Dante."

Luc spoke up. "Ms. Bradley, I'm Dante."

She turned around and offered a shy smile. Then she stepped forward and offered her hand tentatively, as if she wasn't sure he'd accept it.

She was good. Very good. If he hadn't known who she really was he would have assumed he was meeting Celeste Bradley and not Celeste Bradshaw. The direct gaze she'd used on him yesterday had been replaced by an uncertain one. Even the sure way she had of carrying herself had disappeared. She now seemed hesitant.

Even more obvious were the visible changes. He was

surprised by the care she had taken to change her looks. Her blue dress was a simple inexpensive style but with a lower neckline than he imagined she normally wore. Her shoulder-length hair was now clipped shorter in a shaggier style. It looked as if she'd lightened her own dark blond hair color to a much paler blond shade. Bolder makeup finished the look.

The lady deserved a damn Academy Award.

"Let's go back to my office," Luc said, directing her down a small hallway.

Calling it an office was an overstatement since it was about the size of a broom closet. It barely held his desk, a tiny filing cabinet and two chairs.

"Would you like some coffee?" he asked politely.

"No, thank you." She looked around with discreet interest.

Luc stared at Celeste, feeling as if he were looking at an entirely different woman than the one he had met the day before. As he walked past her, he noticed even her perfume had changed. This one hadn't cost a fraction of what the one he'd detected the day before had cost. But it was still something that suited her.

"You said you're a bartender," he prompted, once he'd seated himself behind his desk.

"Yes, sir. I worked as a bartender for about three years when I was in grad school." This time she did meet his gaze squarely. "I have a letter of reference from my boss." She pulled a paper out of her purse and handed it to him.

Luc skimmed the letter, wondering if her partner had written the letter.

"But you haven't worked the past—what?—eighteen months?"

She nodded. "I, uh, I was in jail."

Aha, there was that almost defiant look he'd seen so many times before, even in his own bathroom mirror. She sat there daring him to condemn her for her past.

He'd say *Detective* Celeste Bradshaw was diving way too deep into her part.

"There's no recording equipment in here," he informed her.

"All I want is a chance," Celeste said, as if he hadn't spoken. "I'm a hard worker and I promise I won't betray your trust."

He sighed. Obviously, she wasn't going to fall out of character. "What were you in for?"

She hesitated as if she didn't want to admit the truth. "I wrote a few bad checks."

"Of course you did," he murmured. "All right, I'll put you on a thirty-day trial basis. It's not just me you'll have to convince but everyone else working here. Everyone gets along or the one causing trouble is the one leaving. We don't tolerate drinking on the job. Also there will be no drugs and no horseplay. Your meals are provided free of charge during working hours. We all work together here. As for the bar, keeping it stocked is your job, but my partner, Paulie, does the ordering. Feel free to cut off a customer if he or she has had too much to drink. If they cause trouble, alert me or ask the hostess to come get me. I will take care of any problems that come up. There are two waitresses in the bar on Friday and Saturday nights, one on duty the other nights." He pulled open a file drawer, pulled out a packet and tossed it across the desk toward her. Another packet followed that one. "Paperwork to fill out," he informed her. "There are three ties in here. You provide white shirts and black pants. Nothing tight or low cut."

''Don't your partners have to approve your decision?'' she asked.

''The three of us have an agreement. Jimmy doesn't look at what Paulie and I do, and we stay out of the kitchen. Especially if he's holding one of those big sharp cleavers,'' he said. ''The kitchen is his domain. The paperwork is Paulie's domain.''

''What about your domain?'' Celeste asked. ''What are you in charge of?''

''What is my domain?'' His smile displayed that pantherlike danger. ''Why, Ms. Bradley, my domain is just as important as Jimmy's. I'm the one who makes our customers feel more like guests. Since I gather you still want the job, make sure you're back here at four.''

''I want the job,'' Celeste said firmly.

Luc rose and walked around the desk as Celeste likewise stood up.

''You can meet the others when you come in. Is that acceptable?''

''I'm here to do a job, Mr. Dante,'' she murmured, breaking character for the first time. ''This could very well turn out to be to your benefit.''

''And when this is over, I'll be there to serve you a lovely dish of sautéed crow.'' He spoke equally softly, although he knew there was no one in the hallway to overhear their conversation. His senses always had been finely honed as to what went on around him. He refused to be caught unaware.

She tipped her head back. Clear gray-green eyes stared up at him with an unwavering gaze that seemed to make its way down to his soul. He felt tension coiling deep within his body. He knew he'd never felt this way around a woman before, and he didn't like that he was feeling it now about *this* woman.

"If it turns out I was wrong, I'd prefer no butter on my crow," she replied as she opened the door. "Thank you, Mr. Dante."

Luc watched her leave the restaurant. He had a feeling that the lovely detective was going to be trouble with a capital *T*.

Chapter 2

After moving clothing and personal items into an apartment owned by the police department, Celeste had just enough time to shower and change before making it to the restaurant.

She pulled into a small lot behind Dante's where Gina, the hostess, had told her to park. She noticed it was well lit and easily seen from the kitchen door.

The kitchen was hot and noisy when she stepped in. She garnered a few curious glances, but no one spoke until a beefy-looking man with a colorful tattoo on his bulging biceps showing under the sleeve of his stained white T-shirt approached her.

"You're the new bartender, Celeste, right? I'm Jimmy." He spoke briskly in the raspy voice of a long-time smoker. He didn't bother offering his hand. "Luc said you'd be showing up around now. Someone will cover you around nine for a meal break. Room off to the side where you can eat." He gestured with a thumb

cocked backward. He continued speaking as he returned
to a large pot, dipped a spoon in and examined the
contents while keeping an eye on her. "Luc will show
you how the bar's set up. Anyone in the bar ask about
eats, tell them dining room only except for the peanuts
and pretzels served in there. We're not some sports bar.
What were you in for?"

Celeste feigned embarrassment. "I still had checks in
my checkbook even though my checking account had
been closed."

"Women and their checks." He shook his head.
"Keep your nose clean here and we'll all get along.
Hailey!" His roar was loud enough to make Celeste
wince.

"Guess what, Jimmy, no one's deaf." A woman
wearing a white shirt and black pants moved through
the swinging doors that led to the dining room. She
spied Celeste immediately. "Celeste, right? Luc told us
you're taking Sheri's place. I'm Hailey, as you probably
heard." She shot Jimmy a look filled with censure.
"Actually, you would have heard it even if you'd been
on the other side of the world. The man cooks like a
dream but has no social skills." She led Celeste out of
the kitchen, showed her a room set aside for the employees including lockers for their personal items, then
walked swiftly through the dining room.

Celeste noted the black linen squares set kitty-corner
over snowy white tablecloths and red linen napkins
folded to look like swans set in the middle of white
china plates. Everything about the place bespoke a quiet
elegance. What caught her attention were the crystal
vases on the tables. Each vase displayed a deep red rose
that showed a hint of black along the petal's edges.
Even at a glance, she hazarded a guess they were iden-

tical to the roses Prince Charming left with each victim. She quickened her pace to keep up with Hailey as they walked under an open archway that led into the bar.

Celeste looked around, saw a room made cozy with leafy plants set in corners, round, polished wood tables and comfortable-looking captains chairs with cushions on the seats. A small stage was set up in one corner.

"It all looks so comfortable here, I'm amazed anyone would want to leave," she commented as she inspected the many bottles behind the bar. She noticed nothing was skimped on; even the assortment of fine liquors was impressive.

"Luc wanted a bar where anyone, even a woman alone, could come in and relax without the fear of being harassed," Hailey explained with pride in her voice. She glanced at Celeste. "You'll find it a good place to work."

"I'm just glad to have a job. Some people aren't too enthusiastic about hiring someone with less than impeccable credentials," she said.

"Don't worry, they're great here as long as you're honest with them. I've worked here since the restaurant opened." Hailey cast a critical eye around the room. "There's a carpet sweeper and cleaning rags in a cabinet behind the bar. I'll leave you to get acquainted with everything."

"Thanks." Celeste smiled.

"Thanks, Hailey." Luc walked into the room.

Both women turned. Hailey flashed a bright smile.

"No problem, boss." She left the room.

Luc greeted Celeste. "I'm glad to see you're on time."

"Bosses tend to be more impressed by punctuality,"

Celeste said. ''Is there anything else I need to know before I take my position behind the bar?''

He glanced over his shoulder. ''Why were you questioning Hailey? I thought you already had dossiers on all the employees.''

''I do, and I'm sure you know they don't include everything. And I wasn't questioning her, I was making casual conversation,'' she added. ''When will I meet the last third of the triumvirate?''

''Since you're an employee, you don't need to worry about that. But since I'm sure you expect an answer, I will tell you that Paulie will be in later this evening. As for the bar, it's pretty easy. Most of the clientele are wine drinkers. Mixed drink orders tend to come more often on weekends and at lunch hours. No stinting on mixed drinks, but no overdoing it either. Keep peanut bowls filled. If you're given a mixed drink order you don't recognize, don't fake it. There's a PDA back there that lists pretty much all the mixed drinks. Be polite even if you don't feel like it. As I said before, I'll take care of the rude or drunk customers. We don't believe anyone working here has to take any crap from a customer, no matter who they are.''

''You sound like an avenging angel,'' she quipped.

Celeste was startled by a shift in Luc's expression. She wondered if the hint of raw emotion that flickered across his face was a figment of her imagination. She doubted he would have wanted anyone to see even a suggestion of his innermost thoughts. She had an idea that there were depths to Luc Dante no one had access to. It sparked her curiosity to find out just what those depths held.

By the time the restaurant opened, Celeste had familiarized herself with the bar's inventory and filled the peanut bowls. She was wondering where the waitress was when a brunette whirlwind flew through the archway.

"Hi! You must be Celeste." The woman grinned. "I'm Flip. Actually, it's Philippa, courtesy of my dad. My mom's positive he named me for an ex-girlfriend. It's better than what my mom wanted to name me, though—Eleanor. Can you tell my parents have no sense of imagination? I tell myself it could be worse. There are some really ugly names out there. I believe names have something to do with your personality, don't you?"

"Flip! Take a breath!" Luc's voice came from the entryway.

She stopped and grinned sheepishly. "I've been told I talk too much," she confided.

"I think the reason she makes such good tips is that they pay her to stop talking," Luc said.

Celeste chuckled. "No offense, but you don't look old enough to work in a bar." She gazed at the young woman's dark brown curly ponytail and hint of glitter under two finely arched eyebrows. Even though she was dressed in the same style as Celeste, she looked like a young girl playing dress-up. Celeste noticed the black high heels Flip wore and winced at the idea of spending a long evening on stilts.

"I'm twenty-four." Flip imparted the information with pride as she headed for the end of the bar and sat on a stool.

"If she gets too chatty you'll find the off button on her back," Luc informed Celeste. "Unfortunately, her model didn't come with a mute."

"Ha, very funny." Flip gathered up a handful of peanuts and popped them into her mouth. She didn't wilt under Luc's glare. "I didn't have lunch today, okay?" She turned to Celeste after Luc left. "The man is totally hot but, like my parents, no imagination."

Luckily, Celeste didn't have to worry about a response. Two men in business suits walked in.

"Mr. Haines, Mr. Jackson!" Flip hopped off the stool and walked over to greet them as they chose a table. She returned in record time. "Jack Daniels, neat, for Mr. Haines, and a club soda with a drop of scotch." She leaned across the bar. "Literally, a drop. He's tapering off," she whispered as Celeste poured the requested drinks.

"Always good to hear." She placed the drinks on a tray and watched Flip serve them. She felt she could literally see the energy bottled up inside the young woman as she stood at the table talking to the men.

Celeste couldn't help but notice that the men's eyes didn't stray from her face as she chattered away. It was apparent they knew her well as they questioned her about her classes at college and her life in general—questions she was only too happy to answer. Celeste wasn't surprised that when the two men departed the bar, they left a nice tip.

Celeste found herself busy as the evening progressed. She didn't expect to learn anything useful on her first night, but she did discover she had a useful source. Flip turned out to be a fountain of information about many of the customers.

"Mr. Potter," Flip confided after requesting a scotch and soda, "seems to think we're here to serve him. *We,* as in *women.* He's not rude or anything, just your everyday caveman."

"Do you have any truly strange customers?" Celeste asked.

Flip closed her eyes in thought. "There's strange and then there's strange. No one gets out of hand because they know they could be banned from the restaurant. A few months ago, we had this one guy in who was a total creep. He'd always sit in the corner over there and just watch me." She shivered. "I didn't like the way he looked at me, but I didn't say anything because he never did anything but look."

"But he made you feel uneasy."

Flip nodded. "Big-time. I finally had enough of the way he looked at me and I told Luc about him. He said if the guy ever did anything weird to let him know right away. He also started coming in here more when the guy was here. After a couple weeks, the guy just stopped coming in. He might have been a really good tipper, but I was glad he was gone."

"If he ever comes in, will you point him out to me?" Celeste asked, adding, "Just so I know who to look out for."

"You don't have to worry. He won't be coming back. I guess he came in one day during lunch and started watching Tina who worked the lunch shift. Luc took him off to the side and told him he doesn't tolerate behavior like that. He banned him from the restaurant." Flip picked up her tray and bounced off.

Celeste found herself so busy for the next while that she was surprised when Luc suddenly appeared at her side.

"I'm your replacement for your dinner break," he said. "You'll probably be very happy to spend the next forty-five minutes off your feet."

"My feet hurt more after watching Flip move around in those heels of hers," she replied.

"On any night of the week, she can outdo that bat-
tery-operated pink rabbit," he agreed.

"What's her story?"

"That's for her to say. You better get going if you
want something to eat. Then you can study the kitchen
staff for dangerous individuals," he said wryly.

"It's my job," she said simply before leaving.

Celeste chose a vegetable plate and a couple of warm
dinner rolls. She sat down to her meal with a paperback
novel in one hand. She'd already committed faces to
memory. With the book as a cover, she could eavesdrop
on conversations going on around her.

She heard one of the cook's helpers talk about his
parole officer, another mention he was going to have to
find another apartment and someone else complain that
his girlfriend was talking marriage.

Conversations she could have heard anywhere.

"How's it going?" Hailey asked, pausing in the
doorway.

"Busy, but I like it more that way. Doesn't give me
time to worry I'll make a mistake." Celeste smiled.

"My first night I was so nervous I dropped a salad
in a customer's lap," Hailey confided. "Italian dressing
was everywhere. For some reason, I calmed down after
that."

"At least it wasn't soup," Celeste teased.

The waitress grinned. "Exactly."

Jimmy came over and examined Celeste's plate.
"You a vegetarian?" he asked almost accusingly.

She shook her head. "Since it's so late, I thought I'd
be better off with something lighter. Plus, everything
else smelled so good I was afraid I'd want one of everything."

"Good. Can't understand anyone who doesn't like a

good steak. Hey, don't let that sauce burn!'' He was off and running.

"No joke. If you get a cold, Jimmy makes chicken soup." Hailey grinned before heading back to the bar.

When Celeste returned to her post, she found Luc there having what looked like a confidential conversation with Jared Stryker.

The detective was dressed in his usual thug best. She only had to look at him to know why more than one woman at the police station lusted after him. Worn jeans hugging a rock-hard body topped by a navy crew-neck sweater added to his bad boy image. Light brown hair was tipped with blond from hours on his beloved motorcycle. A battered black leather jacket hung over the back of the stool.

Stryker noticed her first.

"Well, look at the new eye candy," he drawled. "I don't know how you do it, Luc. I'd almost say you had connections."

Luc cocked an eyebrow at Stryker. "It seems I do."

Celeste looked from one to the other. Luc looked like a dark angel too beautiful to resist, while Stryker was just as dangerous in his own way.

"Interesting" was all she said.

"Jared!" Flip squealed, giving him a one-armed hug. "Is he not cute?" she demanded of Celeste. "And don't we look cute together? Except I can't even get him to take me out for coffee." She pouted prettily.

"Sorry, sweetness, I'm way too old for you." Stryker lazily caressed the neck of his beer bottle.

"Flip, work," Luc said quietly.

"You really need to unwind a little," she told him before taking her filled tray and moving toward waiting customers.

"She's not like anyone else working here," Celeste commented.

"Flip's one of a kind," Stryker said. "Like you, Goldilocks. With you serving the drinks, I just might have to lower my standards and come in here more often."

"I'm sure that will make Flip very happy," Celeste said with a bright smile.

Stryker cast a lazy glance in Luc's direction. "If I were you I'd be careful, old friend. Beneath that fluffy exterior lies the heart of a rat terrier." His movements were languid as he climbed off the stool. "See ya later, Luc."

Celeste didn't miss the warning in her colleague's eyes as he sauntered out of the bar. If she wasn't mistaken, she had been silently informed that the two men were close and that she wouldn't want Stryker for an enemy.

She didn't have time to blast a mental reply.

"Go take your break, Flip. We can cover here," she heard Luc tell the young woman.

Barely a minute later, they were alone save for a couple seated at a table across the room.

Celeste picked up a towel and wiped down the bar's surface although it was already clean. It was easier to concentrate on the small task than to feel so aware of Luc standing close by. She told herself that he was the boss watching over the new employee, but there was something about his gaze…. Not that she needed to see his expression to know that. She could feel the hum along her nerve endings.

"So, what have you learned about us so far?" he asked in a low voice. "Any good leads?"

"You know I can't discuss the investigation."

He turned to face her, leaning one elbow on the counter. "You were pretty free with information yesterday when you wanted my cooperation."

"You were only told the basics, nothing more." She turned away and smiled at a man who'd taken one of the stools at the bar. She was aware of Luc's intent regard as she fixed a vodka martini and served it with a smile. "Besides, I'm nothing more than a bartender with a less than impeccable past. Nothing more," she said after the man returned to his table.

"I think you were a woman of mystery even before you reinvented yourself," Luc murmured, then walked away.

By the time the restaurant closed, Celeste felt as if she'd been on her feet for a good twenty-four hours. She hated to think what her feet would have felt like if she'd worn high heels like Flip's instead of the flats she'd wisely chosen.

It's not just cops who are flatfoots, she thought grimly as she closed out the cash register while Flip made sure all the tables were clean. By the time she finished, she could think of nothing more than crawling into bed. Sleep hadn't been plentiful the past couple of nights.

"Celeste, right?" A tall lanky man appeared at the bar. His glasses kept slipping down his nose as if they were too large. "I'm Paulie Connors. If you've finished closing out the register, I'll take the money into the office. Luc did explain that I handle that, right?"

"Yes, he did," Celeste replied, handing over the cash drawer. "He said you do the restaurant's accounting."

He nodded as he took the drawer from her. Skinny wrists protruded from his shirtsleeves.

Celeste thought he looked the part: typical nerd. All

Paulie needed was a pocket protector in his shirt pocket to complete the picture.

''Thanks for filling out your paperwork so promptly. Most of the time I have to practically badger people to get it to me,'' he said. ''See you tomorrow night.'' He turned around and left.

''We're not supposed to go to our cars by ourselves. Luc insists one of the guys always go with us,'' Flip informed Celeste in a confidential tone. ''You heard about that rape a couple nights ago, right? Maybe that guy's sneaking into women's bedrooms now, but that doesn't mean he might not sneak up on someone in a parking lot. I wanted to get a gun.''

''Never a good idea,'' Celeste told her. ''There are too many crimes where people have been killed with their own guns.''

''Yeah, Luc kinda said that, too. He also said it was a great way for me to break a nail,'' she said, examining said digits, which were polished a vivid shade of red. Obviously, the thought of breaking a nail was more traumatic to her than getting shot. ''These babies are all my own and I don't do anything that could do harm to them.''

''That's Flip. Always looking out for herself.'' Luc walked into the bar. ''If you two ladies are ready to leave, I'll walk you to your cars.''

Celeste had hoped to question Flip on her thoughts about the rapist, but Luc's arrival had her postponing it. The young woman had switched her monologue to ''this hot guy I met at Sabins,'' as Luc walked with the two women out into the parking lot.

''I thought you were going to cut down on the club scene,'' Luc commented as he watched her climb into a sleek black Intrepid.

Flip made a face. "I went with friends and stayed out of trouble."

He shook his head.

"See ya tomorrow!" She gunned the engine and took off with a squeal of tires.

"Where does she get all that energy?" Celeste mused as she moved on.

"I don't know, but I could make a fortune bottling it." Luc raised an eyebrow at her vehicle. "Something from the impound lot?"

As Celeste looked up when Luc asked his question, she found herself snared by the darkness of his gaze. Just as before, she felt that tiny bit of warmth settling in the pit of her stomach. What was it about this man that unsettled her so? She quickly shook it off and forced herself back to answering his question before he realized how much he was affecting her. Celeste looked down at the cream-colored Porsche Carrera convertible, deactivated the alarm and slid onto the bucket seat. "Actually, I picked this up at a police auction." She smiled widely. "Good night, Mr. Dante." She took off with a muffled roar.

Luc stuck his hands into his pockets as he watched her drive off.

"When did you take up bodyguard duties?" Jimmy stood in the open doorway as Luc returned to the restaurant.

"I was handy." He walked into the kitchen. Workers were busy cleaning up under Jimmy's sharp eyes.

"Any problems with the new bartender?" Jimmy asked.

Luc shook his head. "She knew what she was doing."

"Did you see the car she's driving? Hell, crime never paid that well for us." The chef chuckled.

Luc's lips curved in a brief smile as he recalled the light in her eyes as she gave him the history of her car. He sensed that she was telling the truth and enjoying it. "It appears we need to shop more at police auctions."

"She got that sex machine at a police auction?" Jimmy roared with laughter. "Guess I better check them out, too. That looks like a sweet ride. Hey! Richie, those pans need to shine." He went after one of the dishwashers. "I wanna see my face in it."

Luc walked through the kitchen and back to the offices. His office was dark, but a light shone in the one next to his. As he expected, Paulie was seated at his laptop computer, his fingers flying with lightning speed over the keys.

"How does tonight look?" he asked, standing in the doorway.

"Very good," Paulie didn't look up from his task. "It's even nicer that the new bartender can actually count higher than ten. I reconciled her drawer first. Not a penny off. Do you know how rare that is? And she had the chore of keeping Flip straight, which we both know ain't all that easy. How did you manage to find her?" He finally looked up.

"She heard about the opening and applied for the job." Luc stepped into the tiny office and dropped into the chair across from Paulie. "She knew her stuff, so I put her on a trial run."

"What'd she do?"

Luc didn't need any further clarification to his friend's question. "Wrote too many bad checks."

Paulie shook his head. "Have you ever thought about hiring someone who doesn't have a record?"

"If it wasn't for Tank hiring us all those years ago, we wouldn't have had a chance in starting this restaurant," Luc reminded him.

"Working in an old diner is a far cry from Dante's Cafe," he pointed out. "It still doesn't mean we have to hire every ex-con that walks in the door."

"Only the ones who can do the work and keep out of trouble." It was on the tip of Luc's tongue to tell Paulie hiring Celeste hadn't been his idea, but he'd made a promise not to tell anyone there, not even his own partners. The promise had left a bad taste in his mouth, but he always believed in keeping his promises. No matter how badly he wanted to break them. "If she can't do the job, she'll be out the door."

Paulie chuckled. "Most men would keep her for her looks alone. But then, you're not like most men."

Luc's expression, or lack of, told Paulie his opinion of his friend's jest.

Paulie shook his head. "We're doing really good, Luc. You can afford to take a night off. Have some kind of life outside the restaurant."

"So can you," Luc said softly.

Paulie ducked his head and busied himself with sorting out sheets of paper. "Jimmy didn't leave the invoices for today's produce delivery on my desk. I better see what he did with them." He rose to his feet.

Since he couldn't easily leave the room as long as Luc was seated in the chair, Luc stood up and walked out into the hallway.

As the two men reached the kitchen, they could hear Jimmy's rough bass as he joked with his helpers.

Luc looked at the two men he considered brothers. Men he considered closer to him than any blood relative could ever have been. Not that he had any blood relatives. The three men's bonds had been forged more than twenty years ago and had strengthened over time.

Luc studied them and the various kitchen helpers working under Jimmy's direction.

He refused to believe any of them could be Prince Charming. But it appeared he would have to suffer Detective Bradshaw's presence until they discovered he was right.

Something about the woman got under his skin. He felt unsettled. Uneasy with himself, and he didn't like that feeling at all.

He wasn't sure any kind of feeling about the woman was a good idea.

After all, she was a cop. And if there was one thing Luc Dante didn't like, it was a police officer.

Even if said police officer was a pretty blonde with shimmering gray-green eyes.

Chapter 3

Celeste struggled to control the yawns tugging at her mouth, but she was losing the battle.

"Hey, Sleeping Beauty, nap time is over," Dylan quipped, dropping on her desk a stack of papers, which landed with a thump.

She looked up. "Tell me this contains Prince Charming's real name."

"We should be so lucky." He picked up her coffee cup and stole a sip. She snatched the cup from his hand.

"Get your own." She set the cup on the other side of the desk away from him.

Dylan dropped into his chair. "So how did last night go?"

"The staff pretty much keep to themselves," she replied. "They're friendly, but they're not going to break down and tell me their life stories within the first hour. I don't expect to hear any confidences any time soon. I will say the restaurant and bar are very well run. I don't know why I haven't been in there before. The food is great.''

"It might have something to do with a sparse social life lately.''

"Look who's talking!''

Dylan ran the palm of his hand over his short-cropped hair. "Got a call from the D.A. earlier. Seems Robinson copped a plea.''

Celeste sat up. "Damn! I was hoping to see him totally trashed in court. Not professional, I know, but that man beat his child so badly the boy was in the hospital for weeks.''

"He's still getting serious prison time. Seems he didn't want his kid testifying against him. Probably the only unselfish thing the bastard ever did,'' Dylan told her.

Celeste shook her head. "More like he knew not only his son's testimony but the scars on his face would bury him big-time. It's times like this that I think about that alternative life I could have. Maybe work on benefit committees, keep an office open for my psychology practice and raise two-point-five adorable children.''

"Don't forget the nanny and pedigreed dog. Maybe you could get one of those poodles with the fancy haircut. Or one of those little dust-mop types that does nothing but yap. Or maybe a cat that lies on a tasseled cushion and looks down her feline nose at the world.'' Dylan pulled three rubber balls out of his desk drawer and started juggling them.

"Bite me, gray fox.'' Celeste used the nickname Dylan had been saddled with since his first day on the force as she picked up the first page and began reading.

She didn't have to read much of the investigator's report to know it didn't offer anything new.

"You know what I can't understand? It rained that night and we still didn't get any viable shoe prints. No unknown hairs or fibers found," Celeste grumbled. "When did criminals get so tidy? My housecleaning service doesn't do this well. This guy could make a fortune as a housecleaner."

"It's all the cop and court shows on TV. Sort of a criminal study course they can take—once they've stolen a TV, that is." Dylan started tossing the balls higher.

"Parker!"

The three balls fell to the floor and bounced underneath Dylan's desk.

Sam stood by Dylan's desk.

"Unless you're planning on running away from home to join the circus, I suggest you leave your balls where they belong," the lieutenant growled.

Celeste's snicker was echoed by the other detectives. At Sam's scowl, the men suddenly showed interest in papers on their desks.

"Give me some good news about Prince Charming," he ordered.

"I called Janice Bowen. She was the first victim. She agreed to talk to us again," Celeste said.

"She wasn't too keen on going over it again," Dylan added, "but Bradshaw used her persuasive skills."

Sam swung from one to the other. "I'll want an immediate report when you return."

"Got it," Celeste promised.

The lieutenant scowled at Dylan, who was in the process of crossing his heart.

"If the two of you weren't such a good pair, I'd split you up. Except I don't dislike anyone enough to make them put up with either of you." He glanced around and took off.

"Next victim," Dylan muttered under his breath.

"Lieu used to have such a great sense of humor," Celeste commented as she stood up and pulled on her jacket. One look at the streaked windows warned her the rain hadn't let up that morning.

"That was before his divorce."

"Your divorce didn't ruin your sense of humor," she reminded him.

"That's because it was the only thing she didn't get out of me." Dylan shrugged on a jacket. "I already signed out a unit for us."

They went downstairs and out the back door. Celeste shivered as the blast of cold damp air hit her face. She quickly buttoned up her jacket over her raspberry-colored wool sweater and tailored navy pants. It never failed—the station was chilly during the winter and warm during the summer, so she'd dressed accordingly.

"Robberies decrease during rainy weather. After all, no legitimate burglar wants to leave what could turn out to be distinctive footprints in mud. Why can't all criminals do the same?" she commented as she slid into the passenger seat. "Then we could stay warm and dry inside the station. All right, dry," she added at Dylan's wry expression. "Maybe this is the year they'll get the heating system updated."

"Stay inside? Are you kidding? If we were stuck inside, Lieu would have us going over the cold cases," Dylan said. "He's said he'd like to see all the cases closed."

"I'm sure he's eagerly awaiting the day when someone will come in to confess to stealing the widow Barker's butter churn back in 1853." Celeste prided herself on having knowledge of the town's older cases, no matter how far back they went.

Dylan adjusted the defroster controls as he rolled out of the parking lot. He lifted his hand in acknowledgment when a patrol car rolled past them.

"That would be a coup. Refresh my memory about Janice Bowen. Was she the legal secretary?"

"Paralegal," Celeste corrected. "She works for Will Zane. Defense attorney extraordinaire."

Dylan muttered his opinion of the criminal attorney who was known to defend anyone who had enough money to afford his services. That he was excellent at his job didn't endear him to the police department. As the attorney stated, if they'd done their job right to begin with, he wouldn't have it so easy getting his clients off.

"It's not her fault she works for a sleaze," she argued.

"Did Zane ever defend any rapists and lose the case? Maybe a disgruntled ex-client decided to take it out on the staff," Dylan said. "We've seen it happen before."

"No one else worked for an attorney." Celeste consulted her notebook. "We have a real estate broker, an artist, a clothing boutique manager and a specialty candle maker. I can't see some guy coming back for revenge just because his candle order didn't come out right."

"You know as well as I do that anything is possible nowadays. Hey! We're the cops, idiot," Dylan groused at a motorist who abruptly cut him off without signaling. "Oughta switch on the lights and siren and see if that gets your attention."

"No macho cop stuff, okay?" Celeste wished she'd brought her coffee with her. Maybe an extra hit of caffeine would perk her up. She had discovered the previous night that it wasn't easy sleeping in a strange bed. The department-owned apartment she was using was generic enough for her cover, but she wished she could have taken more personal items with her to make it feel more like home. Although some of her personal items wouldn't have fit her new persona, she had taken her own bed pillows. They were as important to her as her favorite lipstick and perfume.

"Wish we could have met her at her place or a restaurant instead of her boss's offices," Dylan commented as he parked the car in a circular lot next to a two-story building.

They quickly made their way to the front door, shaking the raindrops off their coats once they reached the lobby.

"May I help you?"

Celeste and Dylan faced a broad-shouldered man, wearing a navy jacket with a security company patch on the front pocket, seated behind a chest-high counter. An electronic gate was the only entrance to the building's pair of elevators.

"We have an appointment with Janice Bowen," Celeste said as she flashed her badge.

The man's face didn't change expression as he studied her badge and identification.

"Does she know you're coming?"

"Why don't you call upstairs and find out," Dylan suggested, baring his teeth just a bit.

The guard hesitated a moment before picking up the phone.

"You had to do that, didn't you," Celeste murmured, turning away from the guard.

"Call it a manly man thing to do," he murmured back.

"No, you just wanted to act like top dog."

"Bow wow."

"Ms. Bowen is expecting you." The guard pressed a button.

The gate buzzed electronically as they passed through it. Celeste was aware of the guard's eyes on them as they walked into the elevator car.

"He was looking at my butt, wasn't he." She heaved a sigh.

"Probably doesn't see too many prime-looking female forms. Zane's usual clients are of the sleazy male variety." Dylan punched the button for the second floor.

"Sleaze that pays well. It lets him own the entire building. I wonder what else he has here. No firm needs a law library that large. And what's the use of him having so many associates when he can still only handle so many cases."

"Doesn't matter. Either way, he makes our lives hell." The car stopped and Dylan waited for Celeste to precede him out.

A woman in her mid-thirties waited by the reception desk. Her posture was defensive—that of someone who was unsure of herself. Her hands, loosely clasped in front of her, twisted nervously.

"Detectives." She greeted them with the barest hint of a smile.

"Janice." Celeste offered her a warm smile meant to reassure. "Is there someplace where we can talk privately?"

She nodded jerkily as she gestured for them to follow her to a conference room filled with a long table and comfortable leather chairs. A credenza sat against one wall holding a water pitcher and glasses along with several coffee carafes and cups. The lush paintings on the walls were obviously original oils.

"Would you care for some coffee or something else to drink?" she asked.

Celeste could tell the woman was asking not out of politeness, but in hopes of putting their talk off as long as possible.

"No, thank you. We're fine." Celeste guided her to one of the chairs. She recalled a picture she'd seen of Janice Bowen at her engagement party. In the picture, Janice's coffee-brown hair had been enriched with golden highlights, her skin was golden from a recent trip to Cancún and her smile had displayed pure joy as she gazed at her fiancé.

It was clear Janice had lost a good twenty pounds from her already slim frame; she no longer bothered highlighting her hair; her skin was the pasty-white of someone who stayed out of the sun; and the elegant diamond solitaire was missing from her left hand. She didn't look miserable, just someone who'd dissociated herself from the world around her. She perched uneasily on the chair near Celeste's.

"Have you caught him?" she asked, her gaze pleading.

"No. I'm sorry." Celeste wished she could have given her the answer she was seeking.

Janice's face fell.

The door opened. "Detectives." Will Zane walked in and sat down next to Janice. She gave him a smile filled with relief.

"Zane," Dylan muttered.

"Mr. Zane." Celeste's greeting was more cordial but still cool. "I'm sure you, of all people, can understand we're here to speak with Ms. Bowen about her case. This isn't anything that requires legal representation.''

''Legal representation is never anything to sneeze at, Detective. I'm merely here to provide moral support for Janice.'' He flashed a smile—the kind any prosecuting attorney knew foretold a legal attack that usually left the prosecutor foundering and the case declared in favor of Zane's client.

No wonder the police weren't fond of him.

Celeste knew many women considered Will Zane a good-looking man. He was an imposing figure in a charcoal chalk-striped Italian designer suit that favored his tall form. She knew there was more than one woman who'd fallen under his spell. She considered herself lucky to be immune to the man's stockpile of charm.

She pointedly ignored a tiny voice that told her she'd be feeling entirely different if he were dark-haired with a dark intense gaze that seemed to see all the way to her soul.

''I understand this is difficult for you, Janice.'' She kept her voice low and comforting. ''But I was hoping if we went over that night again, something might occur to you that hasn't before.''

''All I've tried to do since that night is forget every second, and now you want me to remember?'' Her face twisted. ''Have you ever been raped? Do you have any idea what it's like?''

''No, I don't,'' Celeste admitted. ''But I've talked to enough women to know it's something that will never leave you. That your best closure is to see your attacker caught. That's what we want to do, Janice. We want to find this man and bring him to justice. But the only way we can do it is to sift through every piece of evidence and re-interview everyone involved in hopes something new will come to light.''

Janice blinked rapidly to keep tears at bay. Will got up and walked over to the credenza set against one wall. He poured water into a glass and brought it back to the table. He gently pressed Janice's hands around the glass. She smiled gratefully and took a sip.

''You were in bed asleep,'' Celeste prompted.

Janice nodded. ''I don't know why I woke up,'' she said, each word sounding filled with pain. ''It was as if something brushed across my face. When I opened my eyes, I realized someone was leaning over me.''

''Did you think it was Mark?''

She shook her head. ''He was in Chicago on business,'' she whispered. ''We talked on the phone that evening.'' Janice stared off into space. ''He kept telling me I deserved to be loved. Then he covered my eyes with something.'' Her fingers fluttered by her face.

''When we first talked, you said he only spoke in whispers,'' Celeste said. ''That he didn't speak with an accent.''

''No accent and he never spoke above a whisper. He told me I was beautiful and deserved so much more than I had. Then he lifted my nightgown—'' She choked on the words. ''And he touched me and pushed himself inside me. All the time he kept telling me he loved me.''

Dylan spoke up. ''Yet you never screamed, never tried to fight him.''

Will's green gaze speared them. ''I thought Janice was the victim here.''

Celeste refused to back down under his intimidating stare. ''We need to understand everything. So far, none of the victims has fought back.''

''It's all right,'' Janice assured her boss. ''She's asking what I've asked myself all along. Why didn't I fight or scream.'' She turned back to Celeste. ''So much ran through my mind that night. I was afraid he might be holding a weapon that I couldn't see because of the blindfold. I also hoped that if he got what he came for, he would just finish and leave without hurting me.'' Her hands continued their contortions.

Celeste ached to reach out and grasp the woman's hands, but she knew that many rape victims couldn't bear to be touched. Guessing by the dry-looking skin, Janice also washed her hands a lot. She recalled one victim who took six showers a day because she never felt clean enough.

''I can understand this is very difficult for you, but I'd like you to think back to that night. Was there anything that might have stuck in the back of your mind that you dismissed for one reason or another? Something he might have said to you. Did he wear aftershave or cologne? Was there any kind of odor?''

Janice shook her head. ''I didn't even think about anything, other than praying it would all soon be over.''

Celeste continued her questioning for another five minutes, until she realized she wasn't going to get anything new from the woman.

''Thank you, Janice. We appreciate your seeing us again.'' She closed her notebook and stood up. She glanced at Dylan and Will. ''Gentlemen, would you give us a moment, please?''

Will opened his mouth as if to argue, but Dylan immediately rose and, as if he were the one in charge, ushered the attorney out the door, making sure it was closed behind them.

Janice looked at Celeste with wary eyes.

''I realize your life will never be the same again, but

I'd like to make a suggestion,'' Celeste said quietly. ''Don't hide yourself away, Janice. Don't allow this tragedy to turn you into a frightened shell. The best thing you can do for yourself is to go down to the animal shelter and adopt a dog that can be both a companion and a guardian. Find yourself a big dog with big teeth. You used to enjoy going for runs in the mornings. Take the dog with you or use the indoor track at Sierra Sports Club.'' Sierra was a local fitness center where she knew the law firm had a corporate membership. ''Go out with friends, even if it's for a drink.''

''They can't even look at me,'' Janice admitted miserably. ''They don't know what to say to me.''

''I bet not all of them are that way. Maybe you need to give them a chance. Do not let this man win,'' Celeste urged.

Janice looked down at her bare hands. ''Mark said my 'accident' would hurt his chances at his company.''

Celeste muttered a description that was graphic and less than flattering about Janice's former fiancé. It earned a small smile from Janice.

''Some men are pigs,'' Celeste declared. ''There's someone much better out there for you. But you need to work on going forward. And seek counseling.''

''Why are you telling me all this?'' Janice asked, as Celeste headed for the door.

Celeste paused. ''I don't like to see the bad guys win,'' she explained. ''You're also too intelligent a woman to allow anyone to get the upper hand.''

''How would you know that?''

''You work for Will Zane,'' she said. ''Anyone who can put up with someone that arrogant has to have a strong core.''

The corners of Janice's lips tipped up just a bit. "So you're suggesting I get a big dog?"

"They're the best if you want to go for scare tactics. They're also good company." Celeste smiled. "I knew someone who got a mastiff that was the size of a small truck. Looks mean as could be but is actually a big baby."

When she stepped out into the hallway, Will stood nearby.

"You tell her to get a dog?" Dylan asked, pushing himself away from the wall he was leaning against.

"A big one with lots of teeth. Kind of like her boss." She glanced slyly in Will's direction.

"You asked us to leave just so you could tell her to get a dog?" Will stared at her as if unsure of her motives.

"A dog would give her some confidence because she would feel safer," Celeste explained, tucking her notebook into her jacket pocket. "Thank you for the use of your conference room." She held out her hand.

Will held it a beat too long before releasing it.

"Just catch the son of a bitch," he growled before walking away.

"I was ready to ask if the two of you wanted to be alone," Dylan quipped as they headed for the reception area. "He was looking at you as if you were some juicy morsel of femininity."

"Wow, listen to the pretty words. Have you been reading the dictionary again?"

Dylan's step faltered as a woman walked down the hallway toward them.

With hair the color of wildfire twisted on top of her head and a dark bronze suit accentuating a curvy body, she looked more like a showgirl than an attorney.

"Al." Dylan greeted the woman tonelessly.

She flashed teeth worthy of a great white shark. "Dyl." She mocked his deadpan delivery. She made a production of gazing at her watch. "It's the eighteenth of the month."

"All day."

"I expected something from you in this morning's mail."

"I was assured of a three p.m. delivery." Dylan moved on down the hallway with Celeste right behind him.

"If not, you'll receive a call by three-oh-one," the woman called after him.

"Delivery?" Celeste inquired once they reached the parking lot.

Dylan slapped the top of the car with his palm. "She forgets I have until eleven fifty-nine and fifty-nine seconds p.m. Next time, I just might have it delivered at that exact time."

"Honestly, Dyl, all you have to do is send her a check." Celeste slid into the passenger seat.

Dylan grinned. "Yeah, but that would ruin all my fun."

"What did you come up with this time?" She was familiar with her partner's devious mind when it came to his ex-wife.

"A nice tall cactus in a pot covered with pennies. Ten thousand pennies to be exact." Dylan switched on the windshield wipers to clear off the rain that had collected on the windshield.

"What is it with you two?" She shook her head. "All right, she managed to get alimony when the two of you got divorced, but you don't make it any easier.

If you hadn't ticked off Judge Waggoner when this all started, you wouldn't have had to pay a thing.''

"In the beginning it was a dollar a month," Dylan reminded her.

"And because of your behavior in court, the amount went up," she reminded him. "I bet if you went to Alexa and apologized, she would drop it altogether."

"Yeah, but I'd lose the joy of figuring out ways to pay her her blood money, even though the woman makes a hell of a lot more than I do," he pointed out. "Enough talk about the bloodsucker. Come on, Goldilocks, let's stop for some coffee before heading back to the station." Stryker had bestowed the nickname on her, but the other officers had quickly picked up.

To their surprise, Celeste didn't resent the nickname. She knew in many ways it fit her. Who would expect a sex crimes detective to be a green-eyed blonde who came from a privileged background? She also doubted they would describe her partner, Dylan Parker, aka The Gray Fox, either. Dylan might be in his early thirties, but genetics had him sporting gray hair before he turned twenty-five and intense granite-gray eyes that seemed to see all the way into a person's soul.

From the first day, the duo had meshed as if they'd been partners for years. In no time, they finished each other's sentences, thought alike and sought the same resolution in every case handed to them. They ensured that the victim saw their attacker brought to justice.

"Fine with me. I don't have to be at the restaurant until four for happy hour." A picture of Luc Dante flashed across her mind's eye and a tiny kernel of warmth settled in her stomach. She had an idea the man was going to prove to be trouble for her in more ways than one.

Dylan nodded. "Are you still dating that real estate broker? Bill somebody?"

Celeste slid onto the passenger seat. "Bill Allen? No, we broke up about a month ago."

He glanced in her direction. "Really? He looked like Mr. Perfect to me, even if his pearly whites seemed a little too pearly-white and his handshake was a little too firm."

"He had issues," she explained. "Seems he didn't like the idea that I carry a weapon."

Dylan shook his head. "He knew you were a cop when he first asked you out."

"He asked me if I thought it was a good idea for me to carry a weapon on *those* days," she said drolly.

He chuckled. "And you didn't shoot him?"

"Of course I didn't shoot him. Do you think I wanted to waste my time filling out all that paperwork for discharging my weapon?" She wrinkled her nose. "I don't think so." She looked out the window and thought of the weather reports stating there would be more rain tonight. "How many more before we catch him?" she murmured.

"I don't know, babe," he said. "But I do know that rat terrier personality of yours. That means we'll be hauling the son of a bitch in soon." Dylan backed out of the parking space and headed for the exit.

Celeste thought of what they were up against. Their caseload was increasing. The small police department was growing, but still not fast enough to handle the rapidly growing population in the small town set about a hundred miles north of San Francisco.

Celeste wondered if the good citizens of the town realized just what went on behind some closed doors.

Sometimes she wished she could be as oblivious to the darker side of human nature as they were.

But she knew oblivion wasn't an option, and her nature would have thrust her into any battle.

Chapter 4

Prince Charming isn't a part of this place. Luc would know if that was the case. He would feel it in his bones, all the way down to his very soul. He would feel the dark aura in the surroundings as he had before, and it wasn't there.

Luc didn't see himself as a cynic, but he was well versed in right and wrong. Once upon a time, wrong was a way of life for him. Now he walked the straight and narrow and insisted that anyone who worked for him do the same.

That was the main reason why he refused to believe anyone he worked with would have anything to do with the Prince Charming case.

Luc surveyed the kitchen that was in the midst of its usual predinner chaos, with Jimmy's deep-voiced bellows as accompaniment to the metallic clatter of pans.

Luc looked at the people he considered family. Many of them had worked in the restaurant since the day it opened. Others had been hired later on. His only recent hires were Flip and Celeste.

She's not Detective Bradshaw. When she's here, she's Celeste.

Luc didn't want to think of her as Celeste. He wanted to keep his distance, and the best way to do that was to remember that she was a police detective intent on putting a member of his "family" in prison. And it wouldn't be because someone forgot to report to his or her parole officer, or forgot to pay a traffic ticket. This would be for a vile offense.

Rape.

His stomach twisted at the thought that someone he knew could deliberately attack a woman. He'd read the reports in the newspaper and heard blurbs on TV. This rapist tried to make his victims believe he was making love to them, not attacking them. The thought sent another gallon of acid flowing directly to his stomach.

"Good evening, Mr. Dante."

He turned to find the one person he felt he should avoid at all cost, but whom he found himself moving toward.

"We're pretty informal here," he said, allowing his gaze to feast on her beauty. "Call me Luc." He glanced at the large clock on the kitchen wall. "Right on time."

"I'm working hard to be the perfect employee," Celeste replied with a bright smile as she walked through the dining room.

"Perfect isn't exactly a norm around here." He hadn't meant to, but he found himself following her toward the bar. He stood back and watched her settle in as if she'd worked there for years.

Celeste wasted no time before checking the stock behind the bar, ensuring there were clean towels and glasses. She got busy filling bowls with pretzels and peanuts, as Luc seated himself at the bar. She glanced up and arched an eyebrow in silent question.

"So who did you drag out the rubber hoses and bright lights for today?"

Celeste stopped her task and pushed the bowls to one side. She leaned forward, bracing her forearms on the bar.

"When a cop works undercover, no one should know what he or she is doing," she said in a low voice. "Think of it as a secret."

Luc leaned forward until his mouth almost touched hers. "If there's one thing I can do, it's keep a secret. All I ask is that you don't try to pin this on the wrong person."

Her eyes glittered. Funny, he hadn't thought of a blonde having a temper. Something about this woman showing fire kicked something deep within his belly.

Dammit, the last thing he wanted was to feel an attraction to Detective Celeste Bradshaw.

She was supposed to be cold, hard, unyielding. The kind of cop he had fought against all through his life. Her partner acted like a hard case during their interview—why wasn't she more like him?

Instead she stood there with a smile on her lips, not the least bit intimidated by his scowl.

She smelled like paradise, looked like an angel and...damn, he was looking at her as a woman and not a cop.

He leaned back slowly, as if her proximity had not rattled him.

"If we're going to send someone to jail, we're going to do everything possible to make sure the right person takes the trip and that no defense attorney can get him or her out because we missed something. One thing we do not intend to ever do is arrest the wrong person." She put the containers of peanuts and pretzels back down behind the bar. "Now, if you'll excuse me, *Mr. Dante,* I have work to do." Her cool smile effectively dismissed him.

Luc felt something burn down deep. He wasn't used to this sensation. He prided himself on never raising his voice or losing his temper. And especially, he made sure to never feel too much joy. Experience had taught him it was too easy to lose anything you desired too much.

He pushed himself off the stool and stood up.

"Wow! What a night." Flip seemed to literally fly into the room. "It's pouring outside." She skimmed her hand over her ponytail, which glittered with droplets of water. She stopped short and looked from one to the other. "What's wrong?" Her voice was high pitched and colored with apprehension, as if she sensed the tension as tight as a wire between them.

Celeste was the first to say something. "Salted peanuts versus honey roasted. Which do you prefer?"

Flip looked at Luc, but there was nothing in his expression to give away his thoughts.

"Being a Friday, tonight will be busy," he murmured to her. He looked at the two women. "I'm afraid you're on your own tonight. Angie, the other waitress, couldn't come in. Her little boy is down with the flu."

"Which means I'll be running more and talking less. Got it." The young woman flashed a sunny smile.

The moment Luc left the bar, Flip headed for the bar and took the stool Luc had just vacated.

"Wouldn't he make a great vampire?" she asked Celeste.

Celeste laughed. "What?"

"You know what I mean. He's that dark, dangerous type." She lowered her voice. "He's always so quiet and reserved. I don't think anyone knows all that much about him—even Jimmy and Paulie, and they've been his best friends for like forever," she confided. "It's because of Luc that they have the restaurant. He wanted to live respectably. He once said he wasn't going to do anything stupid that would mean he'd die in prison. Isn't that sad?"

"When you think about it, everyone should think that way," Celeste said casually as she wiped down the bar for something to keep her looking busy.

Flip traced imaginary figures on the wooden surface. "That's what my dad always said. Well, yelled," she clarified. "He doesn't like me much, but that's okay, because I don't think he's all that great either. If my mom had been smart she would have dumped him years ago." Her usually cheerful smile slipped a notch. "It's funny. You always hear that parents say they stay together because of the children. I moved out on my eighteenth birthday and my parents are still together and still fighting. And they wonder why I don't like coming home for the holidays."

"Flip." Celeste reached out to cover her hand with her own. Just then, a couple walked into the bar and took a table.

"Time to work." The darkness left Flip's eyes as she conjured up a bright smile. "Sorry for the angst. Rainy weather seems to do that to me, and we've had way too much rain these past couple weeks." She grabbed a bowl of pretzels as she hopped off the stool, then walked over to the couple. A moment later, she was back with their drink orders and her usual smile and quips.

"Flip, if you ever want to talk…" Celeste offered, feeling sympathy for the young woman.

Flip smiled and shook her head. "Look, you're new here. None of us really talks all that much about ourselves," she explained. "It's like some unspoken rule around here. I don't even know why I told you what I did. Rain has me acting weird sometimes. Just forget anything I said." She took the glasses of white wine and scotch on the rocks and set them on her tray.

You knew it wouldn't be easy, Celeste thought to herself. *It's only the second day.* Yet, she couldn't stop wondering why Flip confessed something so private to her. She wondered if she might not have accidentally hit on a good source for the other employees. She'd noticed the night before that Flip's easygoing nature was readily accepted by the others. She also again wondered what Flip had done to garner her a place at Dante's Cafe.

"Hey, gorgeous, what does a guy have to do to get a drink here?"

Celeste swallowed her sigh. She knew the type only too well. Hair carefully styled even if it was windy and rainy outside, clothing chosen to drape on a gym-honed body and a tan that had nothing to do with the great outdoors. She'd even bet most of those sparkling perfect white teeth were bleached and capped. She brought up the smile she had learned at her mother's knee. The one guaranteed to weaken any man at the knees. It appeared to work on the man seated across from her.

"Just tell me what you want," she said, adding a husky voice to the equation. She set a bowl of peanuts down next to his elbow.

The man's eyes lit up. "Oh, honey, what I want may be behind the bar, but it isn't something to drink."

"Then, you're going to end up pretty dry after you've eaten most of those peanuts."

"Bourbon, neat. You're new here," he commented.

Celeste poured his drink and set it in front of him. Her smile hadn't slipped. "Enjoy your drink, sir." She walked to the end of the bar where Flip stood waiting.

Celeste remembered that when she used to work as a bartender Saturday nights kept her hopping. Admittedly, that bar had catered to the college crowd who were convinced Saturday nights were meant to party.

This Friday-night crowd was older, but it was a constant flow as many guests came in while waiting for a table in the dining room. A four-piece band played bluesy jazz music that affected a part of her deep inside. For a brief second she could imagine herself seated at one of the tables set far back in one of the darker corners. A private table where she and Luc... Shock was an effective cold shower. Where had that idea come from?

Celeste determinedly shook off the disquieting thoughts and returned to her work.

"You've been working nonstop since you arrived," she said when Flip came back with another order.

"If it gets too crazy in here, we can get someone from the dining room to come in and help out," she replied, taking the drinks from Celeste and setting them on her tray.

By midnight, Celeste was fondly thinking of a hot bath, a glass of wine and a good book. On second thought, she just might skip all three and head straight for bed.

At least the bar was quiet, with only a party of four for Flip to look after.

During her dinner break Celeste observed some of her co-workers.

True, they weren't forthcoming about themselves, but she was able to pick up bits and pieces as she discreetly eavesdropped on conversations by pretending interest in the book she had opened the moment she sat down to her meal. By giving the impression she wasn't exactly Miss Congeniality she hoped to prevent their seeing her as a threat.

She didn't expect revelations to jump out at her even the second night, but in her line of work, stranger things had happened.

What felt like an electric wire gone hot across the back of her neck alerted her to Luc's presence.

She had to admit the dark attire suited him. Tonight, black pants and a black silk open-throated shirt had her thinking of Flip's vampire description. She idly wondered how many ladies' necks the man had feasted on. She'd watched him earlier when a party of three couples arrived. Two of the women had looked him over as if they considered him the main course. And if Celeste wasn't mistaken, one had slipped him a piece of paper. She hazarded a guess it was the woman's telephone number. Celeste also noticed that later Luc took the slip of paper, tore it up and threw it away.

Celeste had tried to research his private life, but she hadn't been very successful. All she learned was that he paid all his bills on time, didn't have even a parking ticket against him and kept to himself. Any personal relationships he'd had were usually short-lived. She pegged him as the type that didn't want to be tied down. She could understand that, since he met a great many women in his work. Celeste knew she shouldn't have been looking into Luc's past. He wasn't a suspect in the case. But that hadn't stopped her from indulging her curiosity.

Celeste told herself she wasn't interested in him as a man. She didn't have time for relationships, nor did she want one. Men didn't seem to have an easy time with the realization the woman they were seeing could pretty much whip their butts.

She had a pretty strong sense, however, that her carrying a weapon wouldn't bother Luc Dante one bit. And if she tried to flip him, she'd probably be the one to end up on her back.

A vision of her on her back with Luc looming over her suddenly exploded in her mind.

Celeste quickly set down the glass she held before she dropped it. This was *not* a vision she needed. When she looked down she was disconcerted to see her hands were trembling. To make matters worse, the object of her thoughts was standing right there. She quickly laced her fingers together to hide her unease.

"Survived another night, Ms. Bradley?" he murmured, walking behind the bar. He pulled a bottle of mineral water out of the refrigerator under the bar, opened it, and poured it into an ice-filled glass. He leaned against the bar with one elbow propped on the surface as he sipped his drink.

"Funny, I would have pegged you as a burgundy man," she commented. "Or perhaps a nice merlot."

"I don't drink when I'm working," Luc explained just before he lifted the glass to his lips.

"The intriguing host should at least carry a glass of wine as he moves from table to table greeting the diners," she said. "It fits the image of a debonair man."

"Years ago, the debonair man carried a martini and

smoked cigarettes,'' Luc pointed out. ''Times have changed.''

''Nick Charles,'' Celeste said promptly. ''Those were his trademarks.''

''I thought Nora and Asta were his trademarks.''

''You're familiar with *The Thin Man?*''

He chuckled at her look of surprise. ''Books and movies. Yes, I do read.''

''I wouldn't have pegged you for a mystery reader,'' Celeste replied.

''I have a lot of different interests.''

She cocked her head to one side, studying him. ''Yes, I could see you in a tuxedo, dancing the night away at a nightclub. Spending your afternoons at the racetrack.''

Luc shook his head. ''Not my style. I'm not the idle type.''

She looked around. ''True, no one with an idle nature could have developed this restaurant. You've been successful in creating a place that's elegant yet not intimidating.''

''Intimidation only serves to distance you from the world.'' Luc set his glass down. ''Tell me something, how do you distance yourself from the world?''

''I don't.''

In the dim light his eyes appeared a gleaming black as he slowly studied her. ''Yes, you do,'' he said so softly she could have imagined she only heard the words inside her mind. ''There's a great deal of yourself you don't reveal to anyone because you feel it keeps you safe. You might even see role-playing as the perfect way to go through life. No wonder you quickly volunteered to go undercover. You consider not playing yourself more fun than being yourself.''

''Interesting Psychology 101,'' Celeste murmured.

She didn't want to think how his words could be a little too true. It was easier for her to spar with Luc Dante as Celeste Bradley than deal with him as Celeste Bradshaw. That way, she could do and say anything she wanted and not feel as if she was giving away any part of her own true self. She should have known he would have picked up on her game. He'd already figured out too much about her before. She chose to use humor instead of responding truthfully. "The way I see it is there's nothing like having a dual personality to make life more interesting," she added with a flippant grin.

A faint smile touched Luc's lips.

She guessed the man didn't truly smile all that much. She'd observed him more than once that evening. She had watched him move around the dining room, stopping to speak to diners, and while he always smiled, she sensed it wasn't for real. She wondered if he feared a true smile would be the same as giving away a part of himself. She also sensed he'd been doing it for so long that the defenses he erected were second nature to him.

"Something tells me you are a very dangerous woman, Celeste Bradley." Luc stepped around her and walked out of the room.

"Wow, what was going on between you two?" Flip leaned over the bar after she deposited her tray on the surface.

"He asked me how I was doing." Celeste took the glasses and set them in a rack holding used ones.

Flip rolled her eyes. "It was a heck of a lot more than that. I swear I saw sparks fly off you guys."

"You've been reading too many romances," she said, dismissing her comment. She looked around the room and raised her voice. "Last call, ladies and gentlemen."

Luckily, no one wanted another drink and she was able to quickly clean up while Flip wiped down the tables.

Celeste was just coming out of the ladies' room when she overheard a pair of raised voices coming from the other end of the hallway near the emergency exit.

"You're a pig, Del."

She recognized the strident voice as one belonging to Paula, one of the waitresses. She knew Del worked as one of the busboys.

"You're no saint, Paula," he said, sneering.

Celeste was torn between staying out of sight for further eavesdropping or making her presence known. She opted for the former.

"Let go of me!" Paula ordered, a hint of hysteria in her voice.

Celeste was taking a step forward to intervene when a third voice intruded. She immediately stepped back to stay out of sight.

"Paula, your husband is here to pick you up," Luc said.

From her hiding place, Celeste was able to see Paula disappear around the corner.

"Don't bother coming in tomorrow, Del. Paulie will mail your final check to you," Luc said with a chill in his voice that froze Celeste down to her bones.

"I didn't do anything wrong," the man argued.

Luc's voice grew even colder and harder. "You put your hands on a woman. That's only one of many things we won't tolerate around here. When you were hired, you were told we don't give second chances."

"She was coming on to me."

Celeste silently warned Del to shut his mouth before both feet ended up in there. Literally. She didn't approve of the man's reasoning either, and made a mental note to check out his record again. Maybe she had missed something the first time around.

"No excuses!" Luc's voice lashed out like a whip. "Just get your stuff and get out."

Del left with unspoken threats hanging heavy in the air. Celeste sensed his departure more than saw it.

"You can come out now."

She made her way down the hallway. "I didn't think it was a good idea to intrude," she explained.

The look on Luc's face was almost frightening. There was an anger there she couldn't have imagined coming from someone who seemed so self-controlled.

"It was more than that. You wanted to see if there was a chance you'd found your man," he said wearily. "Believe me, Del isn't the one you're looking for. He was known for liking his sex quite a bit rougher."

"And you hired him?" She was incensed.

Luc's defenses seemed to come up. "He said he had changed. I gave him the chance to prove it. He proved me wrong, so he's out of here." He glanced at the jacket she held. "Are you ready to leave?"

She pulled on her jacket and zipped it up. "Everything's taken care of."

"No problem in you working brunch hours tomorrow?" He walked beside her.

"None. I'll mix up all the mimosas you need." When they reached the rear door, Celeste pulled a roll-brim wool hat out of her pocket and tugged it on before pulling on gloves. The violet color of her hat contrasted with her sun-colored hair. She didn't appear worried it would crush her hairstyle.

"You've got it cockeyed," Luc said, reaching out to adjust the brim of her hat. The backs of his fingers brushed across the curve of her cheek as he fixed the brim.

The sound of Celeste's soft indrawn breath seemed to hang between them as they stared at each other for what could have been seconds or hours. They had no idea how much time elapsed as Luc considered the downy softness of her skin, while Celeste thought of the warmth of his skin against hers as it seemed to send electric shocks all through her.

Could he read her thoughts? Would she ever be able to see beyond the mile-high defenses he'd erected around himself?

She slowly took a step backward to break the spell between them.

"Good night, Luc. Don't let the bedbugs bite," she advised as she walked out to her car.

Luc stood in the doorway, watching her until her car's headlights disappeared from view.

"You're sure turning into parking lot security lately. Are you hot for her?" Jimmy asked, coming up to stand beside his friend. "'Cause she sure is one hot-looking babe."

"Something tells me if you said that to her face, you'd end up with a broken bone or two," Luc told him.

"Hey, she could throw me down for all I care." Jimmy grinned. "Just as long as she falls down on top of me."

"Don't let Emily hear you say that," Luc warned him, mentioning the man's longtime girlfriend. "She'd kick your butt good."

Jimmy shrugged as if it didn't matter to him. Luc knew better. Jimmy might act like a bear with a thorn in his paw most of the time, but down deep he was a softy. Not that anyone would dare say so to his face.

"You know the real reason why Del was ticked off, don't you? He thought he'd have a chance at the bartender job. He wasn't too happy when you hired blondie."

Luc shook his head. "We both know there was no way he would have gotten it."

"Everyone knew that but him." Jimmy clapped him on the shoulder. "Good to see you've got some *cojones* after all."

Luc arched an eyebrow.

"I'm not talking about you having the guts to fire Del. I'm just glad to see you looking at a woman the way a man should. You need to get out more, buddy. Do yourself a favor and break your rules for once. Ask her out."

Luc's laughter held no humor.

"Trust me. That wouldn't be a good idea."

Celeste was thinking more about that hot bath and glass of wine as she unlocked the door to her apartment and stepped inside.

"Hi, honey, I'm home," she called out.

Silence greeted her mocking tone. She headed for the bar that divided the kitchen from the living area. The kitchen light was on, highlighting two tall glass bowls. She walked over and peered into the bowls. One held a multi-finned fish in the deepest jewel tones of bluish-purple with hints of black on his head, the other held a brilliant red fish with touches of turquoise and purple on his flowing tail.

"Hey, Rocky, Bullwinkle, did you guys behave yourselves tonight?" She spoke to them as they swam up to the top. "No wild parties or long distance phone calls?" She picked up a tin of food and gave them each two pieces. They immediately gobbled up their treat. "The perfect roommates. You don't complain if I get home late or if I take too much time in the bathroom. Even better, you don't get into my chocolate stash." She pulled off her jacket and hat as she spoke. "Admittedly, you aren't company the way a dog would be, but you also don't use my shoes for chew toys." She shed her clothing while walking into the bedroom. Normally, she switched on a light since she still wasn't used to the layout of the rooms and tended to hit her shins on the bed. Tonight, though, Celeste preferred to use the light from the kitchen to find her way around the furniture.

As she headed for the bathroom, there was a flicker across the window. Celeste froze. She carefully backed against the wall and hugged the surface as she stealthily made her way toward the side of the window. Keeping out of sight, she carefully glanced out.

The rain made visibility almost nil. If she hadn't been deliberately searching for something out of the ordinary she would have missed what she was looking for.

A few yards to the left of the streetlight outside the building she could see a blurry figure that she sensed had no business being there on a wet night like tonight. She hazarded a guess that the figure wasn't Romeo looking for his Juliet in one of the apartments around here.

Celeste remained at her post for more than twenty minutes before the figure moved away, then seemed to disappear into the rain. She didn't move for another ten minutes. Later, as she undressed, she kept her ears open for any strange sounds coming from the hallway and glanced out her window more than once.

That night she slept very little, even with the knowledge that her weapon was within reach.

He hadn't meant to go there tonight, but he'd been curious about her. He wanted to see where she lived. Did she have a lover? Someone who cared about her? Loved her the way she deserved to be loved? He figured out which apartment window was hers. He hoped he'd have a glimpse of her when she returned home. He knew she was home, he was there ahead of her and watched her go into the building. Why hadn't she turned on her lights? She couldn't have known he was out there. He'd stayed there as long as he dared. The rain proved to be an excellent, although uncomfortable, cover for him. He preferred foggy nights. But as long as he was able to watch over those who needed his protection, he would willingly suffer whatever discomfort he had to, as long as he could make sure she was safe.

No matter. He'd come back another night. Hopefully, the next time he was here it wouldn't still be raining. He hoped he'd have the chance to watch her move around her bedroom while she got ready for bed.

As he drove home he wondered what color her bedroom was and what she slept in and if her skin tasted as good as it looked.

He was positive that when the time came she would give him the same glimpse into heaven he'd experienced with the others.

Chapter 5

"Sunday brunch is nicer when you're partaking of it rather than serving it, even if your task is nothing more than fixing endless pitchers of mimosas and icing countless bottles of champagne," Celeste muttered, handing a cold pitcher filled with a mixture of orange juice and champagne to Flip.

"Cranky," the young woman teased. "Party too much last night?"

"I'm too old to party," she replied. "All I wanted last night was a hot bath and bed."

"You're not that much older than me." Flip added goblets for the drink.

"I gave up partying my junior year in college." Celeste momentarily recalled the reason why, but didn't explain.

"What did you major in?"

"Not partying. Now, go deliver the drinks," she suggested.

Undeterred, Flip delivered the pitcher and goblets into the dining room and returned.

"What was your major?" she persisted, leaning her elbows on the bar.

"Psychology."

Flip nodded. "They say bartending and psychology go together. People will tell their bartenders and hairdressers secrets they won't even tell their spouses," she said sagely.

"The only secret I've learned so far is that Mr. Farr has a sixth toe," Celeste said. "Not exactly earth-shattering."

"I tried college, but it wasn't for me."

She found that curious. The young woman was obviously intelligent, even if she considered an overactive social life her prime objective.

"Why not?"

Flip shrugged. "I don't know. It seemed even the freshmen were too young. They acted like they thought college would change their lives. Maybe it would change some of them, but what I wanted to change wasn't going to happen because of a college diploma."

"What do you want to do with your life?"

Flip shifted from one foot to the other. "You'll laugh."

"No, I won't. I promise." She held up two fingers in the Girl Scouts salute.

Flip looked around to ensure no one would overhear her. "Ever since I can remember I've wanted to be a writer. Not newspaper or magazine articles, but books. I don't expect to write the Great American Novel, just something people can enjoy and maybe even laugh as they read."

"Have you started something?" This did surprise Celeste since she couldn't imagine Flip sitting down long enough to write a paragraph, much less a novel.

She nodded.

Celeste studied her. "Could I read it?"

Flip looked alarmed, as if Celeste had asked her to strip down right then and there.

"You'd want to read what I've written?"

"Once it's published, it'll be read," she reminded her.

"Yes, but it would be read by strangers." Flip chewed the inside of her cheek. "You're serious, you really want to read it?"

Celeste nodded.

She still looked undecided. "I'll think about it."

"I promise I won't correct spelling or punctuation," she teased.

"Ladies, we need some champagne served." Paulie smiled at them.

"My favorite guy." Flip beamed, not looking guilty that she'd been caught chatting instead of working. She moved around to the other side of the bar and picked up a couple of bottles of champagne. "Off to play Champagne Lady."

Celeste gazed at Paulie. She hadn't seen him the previous night even, when she left. She realized that while Luc Dante was quiet, Paulie was downright silent. Paulie was dressed more formally today in a white dress shirt left open at the throat. The sleeves were rolled up to his elbows and navy slacks completed his outfit. She assumed he'd been working in the office and didn't want to dirty the sleeves. His eyes flickered behind his glasses as if he was aware of her regard and not quite sure how to take it.

"Would you like something to drink?" she asked.

"How about some mineral water? Any brand is fine." He hoisted himself up on one of the bar stools. "How are things going?"

"Just fine." She poured mineral water into an ice-filled glass, added a twist of lime and slid it across the bar toward him. "You have trouble-free clientele."

"Which you must not be used to." He waved his hand in the air. "No need to pretend not to hear me. We don't pry into anyone's past here. It's how you are now that counts with us. I've heard you have an excellent knowledge of obscure mixed drinks and you know how to keep a proper distance from the customers. That's a true gift in a bartender."

"You gave me a chance, I'm not stupid enough to screw it up," she told him.

Paulie smiled. "We've all been there, Celeste." He picked up his glass. "Besides, it looks as if you can keep Flip in line. Anyone who can do that is a treasure. She's not the easiest person to be around. Some people have even gotten irritated with her."

Celeste looked over his shoulder to where she could see into the dining room, where Flip circulated among the tables with the champagne bottle. She filled goblets along with a smile and sometimes a word to diners she was obviously familiar with. "She's a lost child looking for acceptance," she murmured.

Paulie nodded at her apt description. "Hopefully, she'll find her way before it's too late." He stood up and picked up his glass. "Mind if I take one of the bowls of peanuts with me?" He reached for the nearby bowl.

"Of course not. It's on the house." She grinned.

Paulie grinned back. He saluted her with the bowl and walked off.

"You do know how to charm the men, don't you, Goldilocks."

Celeste heaved a deep sigh as she looked to her right. "I never thought of you as the brunch type," she remarked, her gaze flicking over Stryker's black T-shirt and jeans. She wondered what it was with some men and black clothing.

"Usually, I'm not, but I like to come in and see you actually working." His grin flashed white in his tanned face.

"Ohmigod, Celeste, I should have warned you more about this guy even if I do have a major crush on him." Flip set the empty bottles on the bar. "He's a cop," she confided. "He's being rude, isn't he?" She made a face at him.

Stryker raised an eyebrow at her description. "Forget to tip just once and they never let you live it down."

"Once? You've *never* given me a tip."

"Did so."

"Did not."

"Did so."

"Did not."

"Grow up," Stryker told her with a broad grin.

"You first," she shot back.

"All right, *children,*" Celeste cut in. "What do you want to drink?" she asked Stryker.

"Whatever's on draft is fine with me."

For a moment, Celeste thought about serving him more foam than beer, then realized it would only make her look as childish as he and Flip had acted.

"Flip, the couple at the corner table are trying to catch your attention," she said quietly. "Don't worry about me. I can handle him."

Flip left, but not without giving Stryker a warning glare.

"How do you do it?" he asked Celeste. "How do you gain someone's trust so easily?"

"I don't have her trust," she corrected. "She thinks she's looking out for me since I'm new here. You're not helping me by showing up here so much."

"Don't worry, I'm practically a regular here. No one will think anything about it as long as you treat me the way you've always treated me. You know, like something you've found on the bottom of your shoe," he clarified.

"I have never treated you that way!" She managed to keep her face composed even as her voice betrayed her displeasure with him.

"No, I guess you haven't." He kept his eyes on her. "Maybe it's because I like yanking your chain. Don't worry, Goldilocks, you're not my type. But I'd say you're the big bad wolf's type."

"What are you—?" She wasn't able to finish her question before Luc stood beside Stryker.

"Don't you have anything better to do than bother my bartender?" he asked Stryker.

The detective swung around, resting his arms behind him on the bar. He finished his beer before speaking. "Hey, Luc."

"I thought you spent your time off out at The Renegade," Luc said, mentioning a bar outside of the city limits well known for its biker clientele and what seemed like fights every hour on the hour.

"I'm going down there later. Had to finish up some paperwork this morning and thought I'd stop by here first." Stryker lowered his voice. "One of your busboys ended up in the drunk tank early this morning. Del Weaver. He decided to have it out with a patrol officer. He passed out the minute he was tossed into the tank, so no chance to make his one phone call.''

''It wouldn't have mattered. I fired him last night and if I hadn't done it then I certainly would have done it now.'' Luc's tone was hard. ''You know my rules. No screwups.''

Stryker nodded. He stood up. ''Walk the straight and narrow, Goldilocks.'' He drummed his fingers on the bar before sauntering out.

Luc turned to Celeste. ''Considering why you're here, I don't feel it's a good idea for your boyfriend to hang around,'' he told her.

''One, I know why I am here. Two, Jared Stryker is definitely not my boyfriend,'' she corrected him. ''He just thinks it's fun to give me a bad time. What he doesn't realize is that the day will come when I decide he needs to be punished.''

''And?''

''And…'' She drew the word out. ''He just might find his beloved motorcycle in pieces. Literally. I happen to be very handy with a screwdriver and a wrench.''

Luc regarded her for so long she had to resist the urge to fidget. The man's attention toward her was unnerving. For a moment, the memory of the figure standing outside her window last night flitted through her mind. She instantly dismissed the idea that it had been Luc Dante. She couldn't imagine he would ever stand outside a woman's apartment building unless it was with the intention to protect that woman. She sensed his very nature wouldn't allow him to even think of doing anything that might frighten a woman.

''Why do you do what you do?'' he asked in a voice

so soft she thought for a second she'd imagined the words.

She carefully arranged her facial features so they wouldn't betray her thoughts. "Because someone has to be willing to speak for those who might not have the strength to do it themselves. And to be there for children who need someone on their side."

His laughter held bitterness instead of humor. "Contrary to what you hear, some children never have the chance to experience the kind of childhood you see on TV sitcoms. Those children learn early on that the men in blue aren't their friends." Like Stryker, he drummed his fingers on the bar's surface before he walked out.

Celeste watched him pause in the reception area and greet a party of three couples. He shook hands with the men, smiled at the women, who each acted as if his smile was meant only for her.

But only she noticed the smile never reached his eyes. She wondered if anyone ever received a genuine smile from him. And she wondered just what had happened to make him so cynical about the world.

Damn her! Luc hung on to his self-control as he spoke to the Allens and their friends. The Allens had been the cafe's first customers and had directed their friends there. He was obliged to spend a few minutes making small talk with them, all the while aware of *Detective* Bradshaw's eyes on him. He didn't have to turn his head to know she was watching him. He felt her gaze like a white-hot brand searing its way all the way to the bone.

Luc was grateful that he could make his way to his office and close the door before anyone decided they needed his assistance. His office might not be large, but then, he didn't need a lot. It was his place to go when he wanted to be alone.

Usually, his reason for seeking solitude was overload from too many people. Today was different. He needed this time because of one person.

He dropped into his chair and just sat there, his fingers idly running back and forth across his mouth.

Celeste was worming her way into him the way no woman had before. It left him feeling uneasy, because he couldn't say he didn't know who and what she was from day one. At the restaurant, she acted her part very well. She was friendly with her co-workers to a point, but made sure she didn't give anything about herself away. If he hadn't known the truth, he'd have sworn her soul was as tainted as everyone else at Dante's Cafe.

Come on, Luc, let's name it after you, Jimmy had suggested when they walked through the empty space that a recently signed lease stated was theirs. *Think of the drawing power a place called Dante's Cafe would have.*

Luc had laughed heartily at his friend's idea. *I'll go along with it just as long as you don't suggest the waitresses dress up like little devils or even angels. Let's not make it too predictable. Let's go for class all the way,* he'd said.

He's right, Luc, Paulie had insisted. *We can do it up elegant the way you said. We can have linen tablecloths, fold the napkins to look like damn swans or maybe even hummingbirds. We'll make a statement, like Jimmy said. Dante's Cafe.*

And that's exactly what they did.

The three men worked hard from the first day. They vowed to give anyone who needed a second chance just that. So far, only one employee had disappointed them. Not a bad track record at all.

And now there was the chance they could lose it all if it turned out Prince Charming had anything to do with the restaurant.

He couldn't blame anyone for not wanting to dine at a restaurant where a known rapist worked.

"Hey, boss." Gina poked her head in. "Paulie said you can't hide in here all day."

He heaved a sigh. "I knew I should have locked that door."

"Then I would have had to pick the lock," she said cheekily. "A customer wants a bottle of that French champagne that costs three hundred dollars, and you have the keys to the cellar."

Luc pulled a key ring out of his jacket pocket and tossed it to her. "Stay out of the cognac."

She wrinkled her nose and muttered, "I'd rather drink motor oil, thank you," as she left, deliberately leaving the door open.

Luc stood up and left the room. He knew it was time to return to what he did best. That was making sure the customers were treated like visiting royalty.

As he passed the archway leading into the bar, he glanced inside. Celeste turned to hand a drink to a customer. Her gaze snagged his.

The woman was proving to be way too much trouble.

Celeste overheard comments about Del all afternoon. Paula's words were the harshest, and since Celeste had been a witness the night before, she understood why. She wondered if there was another way to check him out when she went into the station the next day.

Celeste hadn't worked undercover very much, but she

had quickly resigned herself to the fact that resolution wasn't around the corner and that the crooks didn't come running to her to confess.

"Celeste, that couple over there asked if they could talk to you," Flip said. "He wants a vodka martini with an extra olive and she wants an amaretto and soda."

Celeste looked in the direction Flip was pointing and swallowed her groan. *This wasn't supposed to happen!* She quickly fixed the drinks and set them on a tray. Then she pasted a smile on her lips and walked over to the table.

"What are you doing here?" she asked between gritted teeth while keeping her smile in place.

"Darling, if you need extra money you only need to tap into the trust fund your grandmother left you," the woman said. "As odious a woman as she was, that money really needs to be spent on frivolous items." She looked around. "This is a lovely place. I understand they have excellent food. We're meeting the Bensons for brunch," she confided. "Missy couldn't be on time if her life depended on it."

"We are not related," she informed the couple in a low voice.

"Our daughter asked about you just the other day," the man said, his voice carrying. "When did you start working here?"

"A few days ago." Celeste started to relax but only a bit. She set their drinks on the table. "Did you wish to run a tab?"

"Yes, since we don't know when the rest of our party will be here." He smiled at her after taking a sip of his martini. "Just right."

"Thank you. I learned from an expert," she murmured. "Make sure not to act as if we're related."

"I'll tell our daughter we saw you," her father said with a broad smile.

Aware that Flip's inquisitive nature wouldn't allow her to tamp down her curiosity about the couple, Celeste had her story ready courtesy of her dad's not-so-idle comment.

"I went to school with their daughter," Celeste explained.

"Did you see that ring she was wearing?" Flip's eyes were as large as saucers. "That emerald has to be real, but she was so nice. Not like some of the women who come in here and treat you like some servant or something. She called me 'dear,'" she confided.

"Then, she must like you." Celeste fixed another pitcher of mimosas and handed it to Flip. "Time for you to circulate."

"At least they're all getting their vitamin C," she quipped.

Celeste didn't glance in her parents' direction, and they were kind enough to do the same. She counted herself lucky that the couple that later joined them were unfamiliar to her and didn't look over at her.

When it was time for her break she was grateful they were already seated in the dining room. She filled a glass with orange juice and carried it back to the kitchen.

"There are some food warmers in the break room," Jimmy told her.

"You're feeding the help too well," she said as she found waffles, scrambled eggs and bacon along with a filled coffee urn.

"Nothing worse than a growling stomach."

When Celeste carried her plate into the break room she found two waitresses seated at the table. She hadn't met them before and noted their name badges proclaimed them to be Heidi and Andrea. They glanced at her, then returned to their conversation.

"Norman the freak asked me out again," Heidi said.

Andrea looked up. "When did he do that?"

"Today when he delivered the flowers. He was late with the delivery. Luc had to call him twice. He claimed he overslept." She picked up her coffee cup and sipped the hot liquid. "Just like before, I pretty much told him not in this lifetime, but he doesn't seem to get the message."

"He's sure hooked on you. And here I thought all he cared about was those precious roses and plants of his. He doesn't even want anyone else to put them in the vases. He insists on doing it. He treats them like they're something really rare." Andrea rolled her eyes.

Celeste's ears pricked up at the *R* word. She kept her eyes on her food as if she wasn't listening.

"I'm just hoping he got the message. The guy is downright weird." Heidi shook her head.

"I've seen him when he's taking care of the plants around here. He reminds me of some kind of ugly gnome."

Heidi glanced at Celeste. "If you ever see a creepy-looking guy around and he's talking to the plants, stay far away. If he looks at you, look away. If he speaks to you, pretend you're deaf."

"So this Norman's here every day?" Celeste asked.

"His name isn't Norman," Heidi explained. "I just call him that because he reminds me of Norman Bates. You know, the guy in *Psycho?* For all we know, he has his dead mother in the basement, too!" She laughed.

Andrea nodded. "His name is Carl. He delivers the

roses we have on the tables and takes care of the plants in the restaurant.''

''So he's a florist.'' Celeste tried to sound casual.

Heidi frowned in thought. ''I don't know for sure, I guess so.''

''He has one of those businesses that comes in to take care of plants in business offices and restaurants,'' Andrea explained.

''If he bothers you so much, did you ever tell Luc, Paulie or Jimmy about him?''

Heidi laughed. ''Why? He hasn't done anything other than ask me out and look creepy.'' She blew out an exasperated breath. ''If he gets too pushy I'll say something then.''

''Do you remember that old guy who used to come in for lunch once a week?'' Andrea spoke up. She turned to Celeste. ''He'd always sit at the same table. He'd practically have a fit if someone had already been seated there. He even left Marie a hundred dollar bill for a tip. She told him she couldn't accept so much money. He told her she was worth every penny.''

''Oh, him!'' Heidi groaned with a laugh. ''He made us feel so uncomfortable that we finally told Luc. Luc banned him from the restaurant.''

''I would think that upset him a great deal.'' Celeste made mental notes. Now she had someone else to check out.

''Luc called him at his home and told him he would no longer be welcome at the restaurant,'' Heidi told her. ''The next day this guy shows up for lunch. Gina told him she couldn't seat him and he started yelling at her. Luckily, Luc was here, because Paulie doesn't have the balls to deal with someone like that. I don't know what

Luc said to the guy, but it was enough that he never came back.''

"When did this happen?" Celeste asked.

Heidi and Andrea looked at each other.

"When was it, eight, nine months ago?" Andrea looked to her friend for confirmation.

Heidi nodded. "I was working the lunch shift that day, too," she told Celeste. "This guy came so unhinged I thought he was going to deck Luc. Which has to mean he's nuts because no one in their right mind would try to hit him."

"Gee, I had no idea there were so many creeps out there. First I hear about Del, now these guys." Celeste shook her head in wonder.

"Around here they're few and far between," Andrea assured her. "Just goes to show that even upscale places get sleazoids at times." She glanced at her watch. "Time for me to get back. At least we're only open until six on Sundays." She stood up.

Celeste finished her food. After taking her plates into the kitchen, she stopped at the open back door. She noticed the rain had stopped, leaving the sky overcast and gray. She stood there breathing in the damp fresh air. When she started to turn away she noticed a dark figure standing under the building's overhang. A bright spark illuminated his features.

She stood there for several minutes just watching him. She'd read about a man seeming to radiate loneliness. Looking at Luc, she actually saw what the word meant. She sensed he wasn't as comfortable with his loneliness as he thought he was.

She pushed open the screen door and carefully made her way down the side of the building. Luc continued looking out into the wet parking lot. He held a glowing cigarette in one hand.

"A habit I've been trying to break for some time," he said, dropping the cigarette to the ground and grinding it with his foot. He stooped down to pick up the crushed cigarette butt. "What about you?"

"I tried smoking when I was in high school. Took one puff and...let's just say that was my last." She could hear her teeth chattering in the cold air. She was surprised he wasn't shivering, since he wasn't wearing a jacket. "You must be desperate if you're out here in this weather."

"It stopped raining a few minutes ago."

"I have some questions," she said, thinking of her conversation with the two waitresses.

"Work related?"

"Not exactly, and nothing I'd like anyone to overhear."

"Of course," he mocked her. "Fine. You'll find me at two-seventeen Ross Street around eight." He stepped around her and walked back to the door. "You might want to think about getting back inside before you catch a cold," he advised over his shoulder. "We can't afford to lose another bartender so soon."

Celeste watched Luc walk back to the kitchen door. Damn, the man even looked good walking away. She sighed when the rain started up again the moment he stepped into the kitchen.

"Even the elements seem to be on his side," she muttered, running for the door.

Chapter 6

Ordinarily, Luc wouldn't have expected Celeste to take him up on his impulsive invitation. He still had no idea why he had told her to meet him, unless there was something in that cigarette that shouldn't have been there.

But he knew if she did show up, she'd be there on time. And just like a finely tuned watch, she was dead-on. What surprised him was her expression when she entered the restaurant. Or lack of it, considering her surroundings.

Damn her, she actually fit in.

Tonight, she was dressed casually in hiking boots, faded jeans, a dusty green marled yarn crew-neck sweater and a denim jacket. Her hair was damp from the fine mist that had been falling for the past hour, and her only makeup was a touch of lip gloss.

His breath caught in his throat as he watched her stand in the doorway while taking off her jacket. Dammit, why did she have to look like someone who could save his black soul?

Celeste looked around the small diner until she spied Luc seated in the rear booth. She walked back to him.

She hadn't expected him to choose a diner that, on the outside, looked as if it had existed in better days. If it hadn't been for the lights glowing inside, she would have thought it was permanently closed.

She told herself she was meeting him because of the case, but she couldn't lie even to herself. She was here because of Luc Dante. She hoped she might learn a little more about the man.

"They need more streetlights around here," she said by way of greeting, sliding into the seat across from him. "I almost missed it. You didn't give me the name of the diner."

One corner of Luc's lips tipped upward. "He likes to remain low-key."

She nodded. "Ah, that explains the lack of a sign out front."

"Coffee?" a man behind the counter yelled at her.

To her credit, she didn't jump at the raspy shout directed at her. She turned and smiled. "Perfect timing— I could really use a cup."

"We ain't got any of those flavored creamers you dames like," he warned her.

"Good. I prefer mine black and strong enough to float the entire U.S. Navy."

The man poured coffee into a heavy white ceramic mug and brought it over.

Luc admired the way she didn't bat an eyelash as Tank set the mug in front of her. Tank had even deliberately used the silver hook that had replaced his hand more than thirty years ago. The food-stained apron covering a white T-shirt and white cotton pants announced him as the cook. The tattoos of naked women adorning his beefy arms and the scowl on a face battered by one too many fights made him a formidable figure.

Luc made the introductions. "Celeste, this is Tank."

"Hi." She looked up at the tall man and smiled.

"You want anything to eat?" Tank asked her.

Celeste picked up the plastic-coated menu and scanned the offerings.

"I'll have the cheeseburger," she decided.

He looked at her suspiciously. "Onions?"

"Of course," she said promptly. "Raw, not grilled, please."

He glanced at Luc as he turned away. "Don't see manners in here too much."

Celeste wasn't too sure if it was a compliment or not. She wasn't about to ask.

He didn't bother to write down her order before returning to the kitchen. A moment later, they could hear the searing sound of meat hitting the surface of a hot grill.

Celeste looked at Luc, who only had a cup of coffee in front of him. "You're not eating?"

"Tank already has my order," he replied.

"Let me guess. He was in the Marines." She nodded toward the black-and-white photographs on the walls along with a colored drawing of the Marine Corps mascot, the bulldog, near the door.

"He was a drill instructor, and from what I heard he was a recruit's worst nightmare during boot camp. Where's your partner?"

"Probably on a hot date. Why, was I supposed to bring him?" She looked amused. "I know it's hard to believe, but there are times when I'm allowed out after dark on my own.''

''The way you talked about questions, I figured it had to do with the case and he'd be coming with you,'' he replied.

''I'll fill Dylan in tomorrow.'' She picked up her coffee mug and sipped the hot liquid. ''Whew! This must have been on the burner since last year.'' She took another sip.

''What questions do you have?'' Luc wasn't in the mood for small talk.

Celeste ignored his almost surly behavior. She hadn't missed the expression on his face when she walked toward him. He hadn't been sure she'd show up. It felt good to put him off balance for once.

''A couple of the waitresses were talking about the man who delivers the roses you put on the tables,'' she said.

Luc shrugged. ''Carl? What about him?''

''It seems he's been a little persistent in asking one of them out. Even going so far as getting pushy at times. He would have access to the same roses that are left at the crime scenes,'' she continued. ''The waitresses also mentioned a former customer of yours who had a habit of leaving hundred dollar tips.''

Luc closed his eyes and muttered a curse. ''Woodrow Taylor. He's nothing more than the clichéd dirty old man. He's probably in his late seventies. He likes to look down women's tops. When he was coming in, the waitresses wore a different type of shirt. More like a round-necked top. It wasn't all that low cut but he started making some of the waitresses feel uncomfortable. After that, I suggested to Paulie and Jimmy that we come up with something more conservative. Taylor was told he was permanently barred from the restaurant. He threatened to sue. I reminded him that we reserve the right to refuse service to anyone and we would definitely refuse to serve him. He's probably making the rounds of other restaurants.''

''And the florist?'' she persisted. ''What about him?''

''Carl is a plant care specialist, not a florist,'' Luc explained. ''He works for a lot of small businesses in town. He fixes up floral displays on a weekly basis for some offices and supplies greenery for others. He was able to give us an excellent price for the roses, so we get them from him and he takes care of the plants we have. I can't imagine Carl being the one. He's one of those shy guys who would run the other way if a woman even talked to him.''

''For someone who's that shy, it's surprising he got up the nerve to ask someone for a date, isn't it?''

''Here ya go.'' Plates were slid in front of them. Squeeze bottles of ketchup, spicy brown mustard and hamburger relish were plopped down in the middle of the table. Tank scowled at Celeste. ''You want more coffee?''

''Please, and do you have any barbecue sauce?''

His brow furrowed in suspicion. ''For what?''

''I like to dunk my French fries in barbecue sauce,'' she replied. ''It's tastier than ketchup.''

''Yeah, I got that,'' he growled before stomping off and returning with a bowl of barbecue sauce.

''Thank you.'' She turned back to Luc. ''Well?'' She picked up a fry, dunked it in the barbecue sauce and nibbled on it.

He took his time adding mustard and relish to his burger and took a bite before replying. ''Carl's not a viable suspect.''

"Viable suspect," she murmured. "Gee, Mr. Dante, you sound just like a cop."

His dark scowl was worthy of Tank.

"Look, I already know no matter what I say, you'll investigate Carl anyway. Waste your time if you want. You won't find a thing on him," he told her, taking another bite of his burger.

"I do value your input, but I still intend to check him out." She did the same. "This is really good," she said, taking a second bite. "I can't believe I've missed this place."

"It's not exactly four star," he reminded her.

"Hell, I'm not even one star," Tank boomed with a deep rumbling laugh. He sounded proud.

"Don't you have a kitchen to clean?" Luc asked.

"It's not going anywhere. It's a hell of a lot more fun listening to you two. So what is she? She sounds like a cop. I get a lot of cops in here. Haven't seen her before." Tank walked over and refilled their coffee cups. He looked at Celeste. "You don't look like a cop."

"Tank," Luc warned.

The man shrugged good-naturedly as he walked off.

Luc turned back to Celeste. "Who else do you want to dissect?"

"For now, that's pretty much it," she admitted. "I have to follow every lead. At least I talked to you first before I started my digging."

"And that's supposed to make me feel better? You don't care about my opinion. You'll do what you want to do because you already have me by the ba—shorts," he quickly amended.

She stared at him with expressive eyes. "Did the System hurt you that much, Luc?"

He didn't need to ask her what she meant. He tossed his napkin on his plate and slid out of the booth.

"The lady's paying, Tank," he called out as he left the diner.

"Damn him!" She pulled bills out of her jacket pocket, dropped them on the table and took off after him. "Luc!" She pushed the door open and ran outside.

He'd just reached his vehicle when she caught up with him.

"What is your problem? Are you even going to tell me what I supposedly did in there? Did I hit some kind of nerve?" she demanded.

He hit the remote. Headlights flashed as the door locks disengaged.

"Just leave it, Detective," Luc ordered, not bothering to turn around.

"Leave what?" She stalked up to him. "Come on, Dante, give me a clue!" she yelled. "Do us both a favor and tell me what your problem is!"

Luc spun around and grasped Celeste by the shoulders. Before she could blink she was backed up against his car.

"Guess what, Detective?" he growled, deliberately pressing his hips against her. "*You* are my problem. You have been my problem since that first meeting, with those smiles and big eyes and..." His eyes found her lips. He muttered a curse just as he dropped his head and captured her mouth with his.

OhmiGod!

Celeste felt as if her breath had been slammed out of her body. While the night air was chilly and a fine mist fell from the sky, she didn't feel the least bit cold with the heat of Luc's body against her.

She couldn't think. She could only feel. And what a feeling it was!

Was this what she'd been unconsciously waiting for since that first meeting? Had she known that by coming here to talk to him there was a chance this could happen?

She didn't have to order her arms to curl up around his neck. They moved upward of their own accord just as she arched against his body.

The man might act cool and aloof, but there was a heat inside him that seared her. It was as if he called out to something deep inside her.

There was a connection racing between them she couldn't understand, but she was powerless to deny it.

"Now you know my problem," Luc rasped as his mouth moved up across her cheekbones, then returned to her mouth with a hunger that seemed savage. His fingers dug into her scalp, holding her head still. Not that she could have moved if she wanted to. And she most definitely didn't want to. "You have been like an intense heat that scorches my skin. It refuses to go away. You tell me how that can happen in the space of days?" he demanded, pulling back on her head until she could look up at him. His face twisted as if he were in pain. "Damn, why did you have to barge into my life?"

Her breath caught in her throat as she saw the starkness of his gaze. The man was fighting his emotions every step of the way and not liking where they were taking him. Her normally glib tongue escaped her. What could she say when she had no idea what was happening to her either?

"I don't know," she finally had to confess. "All I do know is that if you don't kiss me again I will die."

Luc groaned and caught her mouth with his. His tongue plunged in, mingling their flavors. Both were so involved that they wouldn't have cared less if they'd been in the middle of a football stadium during the Super Bowl. She gasped and arched her back as his hand curved over her breast. She suddenly wanted nothing between them as she nibbled on the corners of his mouth. He retaliated with a love nip of his own. At that moment, nothing could have pulled them apart.

Until a popular cartoon theme song erupted between them.

It took Celeste a moment to register that it was her personal cell phone.

"I have to answer it." She reluctantly pulled back. She flipped open her phone. "Hello?"

The voice speaking from the other end broke the mood faster than an icy downpour.

"Mom?" she croaked.

Luc jumped back as if he had been burned.

Celeste turned around. She curved her arm around her waist as she listened to her mother.

"Mom, can I call you back later? No, I'm not on duty tonight. I'm just...busy. Who?" She tipped her head back, silently beseeching the heavens to save her. There was no help there. She grimaced. "Mom, I can't talk right now, okay? I will call you later." She lowered her voice. "No, I do not want his number. He was a pompous jerk in school and I'm sure he hasn't changed even if his company did go public." She disconnected the call.

"Sorry about that. I should have checked my caller ID first. Then I would have known it wasn't the station." When she turned around she found Luc leaning against his car. His shoulders shook. She peered closer.

The parking lot lights showed up his features in stark detail. "Are you laughing?"

"Hard to believe, isn't it?" he said dryly. "Obviously, you weren't about to tell your mother what you were doing."

"Not for the reason you think. She'd be so happy I was doing more than frisking a suspect she'd demand I bring you for dinner." She rubbed her hands over her face. As she did so, she realized she could smell him on her palms. She noticed Tank standing at one of the front windows. Well, what could she expect? They were probably as good an entertainment as he could find on cable. She couldn't believe she wasn't embarrassed by what was probably a pretty good R-rated scene.

"I have to go," she murmured, searching her pockets for her keys. All the time, she was intensely aware of Luc's brooding gaze on her.

"If you want to send your partner in Tuesday night, I'll understand."

Celeste swung around. "I don't run away from anything."

"So now what? You'll investigate some guy and make his life miserable because you've decided he could be Prince Charming?" Luc asked.

"There are some aspects to the case we can't let anyone know." She fell back into her cop persona. Right now, when she still felt so unsettled, she needed that defense. She wondered where it had been ten minutes ago.

This time his smile was chilling. "Of course." He straightened up and turned to his car. "Good night, Detective."

Just like that.

In the space of seconds she saw the return of the man

she had seen for the past few nights. There was no sign of the heat that had radiated off him just moments before.

Celeste called on reserves from deep within her. She refused to allow Luc to see how his emotional withdrawal affected her.

"Good night, Mr. Dante." Her voice was as cool as his had been. "I hope you will remember that anything we discussed tonight cannot be disclosed to anyone."

"Don't worry, I wouldn't dream of doing anything to hinder your investigation."

Celeste ignored his mocking voice and headed for her car. She started it up immediately. She ignored the cold air that blew on her when she first switched on the heater. At the moment, nothing could be any colder than the chill she felt inside.

He'd always considered himself a damned man. Tonight proved it.

Luc had no idea why he'd given in to his baser side and kissed Celeste. Maybe because it was something he'd imagined doing for several days. Or maybe because he'd followed through on what he'd dreamed about since he first laid eyes on her.

He drove blindly. At the moment, he didn't care where he went. When he reached the outskirts of town, the mist changed to heavy rain. That didn't matter either. If he drove fast enough, he just might be able to escape the images and sensations that haunted him. And if he slid off the road, it was meant to be.

The dazed look in her eyes took him back to a stormy night that equaled the storm inside him.

He thought back to when he was fourteen and he'd hitchhiked to San Francisco, and from there farther down the coast. He recalled standing on the beach for hours, where he watched a storm roll in from the ocean. He remembered the water was green, dulled by the storm-gray clouds overhead. As he stood there, he felt the power of the storm as it advanced onto the land, and imagined he heard the crackle of electricity in the air as lightning lit up the sky.

To this day, he couldn't forget all the hours he spent on the beach or how watching, and feeling, all that turbulent energy affected him.

The cops picked him up two days later and returned him to the Watsons. Two days later, he was in the Valley Boy's Facility, just another fancy name for juvenile hall.

Tonight, Celeste's eyes had reminded Luc of the stormy sea. What raced through him at her touch was the same sense of electric energy he'd felt then. And just like that day, it scared the hell out of him.

He didn't stop driving until he saw flickering lights in the distance. He later pulled off the road and parked near the one-story building. Even with the pounding rain and all his windows closed, he could hear the vibrations of the music and Jim Croce's raspy voice booming from the rough-hewn log building ringed with motorcycles.

Luc climbed out of his car and walked inside. He didn't bother setting the car alarm. He had no fear of his powerful car being stolen. There was no chance of anyone wanting his sleek sports car when there was a wealth of Harley-Davidsons close by.

When he stepped inside the building, he was assaulted with sounds, sights and smells. Jim Croce had been replaced by the heavy throbbing beat of Steppenwolf. Leather and denim was the accepted dress code among the too many overheated bodies, and beer the drink of the day. Smoking may have been banned from bars, but no one heeded that law in The Renegade. It could have been an outlaw saloon from a hundred and fifty years ago.

He waded through the pack of bodies and snagged one of the few empty stools at the bar.

"Well, well, well, look what the rain brought in." Jared Stryker slapped his palms down on the other side of the bar. Unlike the polished wood surface at Dante's Cafe, this bar's surface was scarred from burning cigarettes, wet glasses and bottles and just plain time. "What'll you have?"

"Whatever you have on draft."

"Good choice." He drew a mug and slid it over to him. "Dealing with all those fancy customers must wear a guy out. You look like a train ran over you." Stryker peered at him closely, then sniffed. "Damn, you've been with Goldilocks."

Luc's two-word retort was graphic and to the point.

"No thanks, you're not my type." Stryker was unfazed. "Just as I'd think the lady wouldn't be your type." He shot Luc a meaningful look.

Luc drank the beer and now wished he'd asked for something stronger. "I thought you guys weren't allowed to moonlight." He knew changing the subject wouldn't work, but it might buy him a few minutes to organize his thoughts.

"I'm here checking out a few people," Stryker murmured. "Besides, I like tending bar out here. If it gets too rough I can knock a couple heads together and no one gets pissy with me."

Luc picked up his beer and drank. "Why do they think my place is a connection? What brought it up?"

The detective glanced around to make sure no one was listening. The Renegade was known for people minding their own business, but some people would do anything for information.

"I don't work domestic and sex crimes," Stryker replied in a low voice.

"Why does she?" There was no need for him to clarify his question.

"Ask her." At the shouted request for a beer, Stryker opened a bottle and slid it down the bar with practiced ease. "Damn, this job is so easy," he commented. "Tips suck, though." He turned back to Luc. "She's strictly uptown. Her dad's a big-time estate developer with connections in Sacramento and D.C., her mom's got one of those platinum pedigrees that goes back to the dawn of man. Goldilocks should be one of those pampered little darlings I used to bust all the time when I was in uniform. It's not her style. She worked her cute little butt off when she worked patrol, and when the town started growing like wildfire and the department with it, she fought hard to start up a domestic and sex crimes department. Her private life is kept just that. There's been talk that she and her partner have hit the sheets a time or two, but it's always been nothing more than talk. No one really knows for sure."

Luc rolled the idea over in his mind and instantly dismissed it. She wouldn't have responded to him the way she had if there was a lover in the background. He'd also seen the two of them together, and no matter how well two people might cover up an affair, there were always small signs. He hadn't seen any.

But he'd sure felt something when she kissed him back. No wonder he'd felt as if someone had literally knocked him off his feet. The lady packed quite a punch with her kisses.

Stryker leaned over the bar, resting his forearms on the scarred wooden surface.

"So, I'll ask again. If you were with a tasty morsel like Goldilocks, why are you here now?"

Luc didn't say a word.

Stryker shrugged. "Look, Luc, I may give the lady a hard time, but I can tell you that she's a straight shooter. She doesn't lie, she doesn't use her looks to achieve her goal and she fights for the victims. If she and Parker feel there's a connection to your place, then there has to be one." He held up his hand to ask for silence as he anticipated his friend's argument. "I'm not saying it's someone working there. Think about it, Luc. You have a lot of people coming and going. Who says it isn't one of your customers?"

Luc shook his head. "I don't want to think someone I know would do something like that."

"No one does." Stryker opened a bottle of beer and drank deeply. "Six months ago I arrested a guy who had decided he didn't want to be married anymore but didn't want to pay for a divorce. He thought he'd committed the perfect crime. Now he knows that no matter how many times you clean a hardwood floor, blood residue remains."

Luc looked at the man who had grown up on the streets as he had. Been the same kind of hell-raiser.

"I never would have figured you turning into a cop."

"Same here. When Judge "Hard-Ass" Hardisty gave me the choice of the army or jail and I chose the army, I didn't expect to end up an MP." He chuckled. "Do you know that bastard is claiming if it wasn't for him I'd probably be doing twenty to life if not sitting on

Death Row right now? Damn him, he's probably right. At least you took the easier route by straightening yourself out without Hard-Ass after you.''

"Only because I didn't want to do twenty to life either." Luc looked around for the tavern owner. "Where's Lea?''

"About as sick as someone can get when they catch the flu. I told her I'd help out tonight since I was off." Stryker indicated Luc's mug, silently asking if he wanted another.

Luc shook his head as he dropped a few bills on the bar. "It wouldn't be a good idea for one of the owners of Dante's Cafe to be picked up for drunk driving," he said. "I've got enough to worry about as it is."

Stryker nodded. "I'd say you're probably the only one around here worried about a DUI. I can tell you one thing, Luc. They're playing this case close to the vest. If it turns out your place isn't a connection, they'll make sure no one will ever know they checked the place out."

"Yeah, well, we'll see just how good their word is." He slid off the stool.

"You never did say why you're sitting here talking to me when you could be off somewhere making cozy with you-know-who."

Luc knew his grin was more lighthearted than he'd felt in some time.

"You're right, I didn't."

Chapter 7

"Here you are. Everything you've ever wanted to know about Carl Thatcher and were afraid to ask," Dylan reported, tossing two sheets of paper onto Celeste's desk. "Other than he and his mother owning Thatcher's Trees and Flowers and his being a member in good standing of the Better Business Bureau, the man literally has no life."

"His mother," she murmured, picking up the paper and scanning it. "Heidi calls him Norman the Freak because he reminds her of Norman Bates. She even made a joke that she wouldn't be surprised if he keeps his dead mother in the basement."

Dylan dropped into his chair. "No, Mommy Dearest is alive and well. The man is so clean he squeaks. He hasn't gotten so much as a parking ticket. His mother, on the other hand, is a piece of work." He held up another sheet of paper with a theatrical flourish. "Disturbing the peace, drunk and disorderly, destruction of public property. She hates pretty much everyone, including her son, who doesn't have the guts to move out of her house. He's manager of the plant business that his dad opened more than forty years ago. Mama claims everyone's out to cheat her, even her son. She keeps a close eye on him and a tight fist on the purse strings.''

Celeste took the paper from him and quickly scanned the contents.

''I would think a mother like that would have you hating women, not claiming to love them.''

''Maybe he's looking for the love he doesn't get at home. One interesting tidbit I picked up while checking him out—I found out the name of the rose he delivers to the restaurant.'' He wiggled his eyebrows.

''You have been busy this morning. I'm proud of you.''

Dylan dipped his head in acknowledgment. ''Drum roll, please.'' He mimicked the motion. ''Deceptive Beauty.''

''Deceptive Beauty,'' she repeated. ''Very appropriate. You know, we really should go out and have a chat with Carl.''

''What if he recognizes you?''

Celeste shook her head. ''As far as I know, he hasn't been in there when I'm working. He goes in about an hour before the restaurant opens. I doubt he'd make a connection anyway.''

''Then, I agree. Let's go out and talk to the guy.'' Dylan pushed himself out of his chair and grabbed his jacket.

''Detectives.'' Sam Adams paused by their desks. He speared them with the gaze his detectives called downright scary. ''Tell me you have something. Anything.''

''A caveman pretending to be a busboy who's been

a little too grabby with the waitresses,'' Celeste replied. ''And the man who provides the restaurant with the roses isn't too popular with the waitresses either. They consider him a freak.''

His mouth thinned with displeasure. ''You call those leads?''

''I've only been there three nights, sir,'' she explained. ''I'm lucky to have learned what I have so far.''

''I don't want this guy striking again.'' He made it sound like an order.

''Neither do we,'' Dylan told him with grim determination.

Sam nodded and moved on.

''At least we still have our butts,'' Dylan muttered, steering Celeste out of the building and down to the garage. ''You haven't said too much this morning. Rough night?''

She kept her eyes trained ahead. ''Just the usual. Except my parents showed up yesterday during brunch.''

''Parents usually don't show up when someone's working undercover.'' Dylan signed out for an unmarked unit, then tossed the keys up into the air and caught them behind his back.

''Stryker showed up, too. At least my dad leaves a tip.''

''The object of working undercover is that no one finds out your true identity. That isn't too easy to accomplish when family members show up. But then, I never have that problem.''

''Of course you don't,'' she pointed out. ''When you work undercover, you deal with porn producers. Along with that guy who was producing kiddie videos.''

''That was one bastard I was happy to arrest,'' Dylan snarled.

''There was also Rosanna Doretsky,'' she reminded him. ''She thought you were hot stuff.''

''And I thought she was all woman until I found out otherwise when I frisked her for weapons. Damn, she made a good-looking woman, too.'' Dylan punched in a code and waited for the gate to roll back before pulling out onto the street. ''What's the address of Thatcher's place again?''

She glanced down at her notebook. ''One-twelve Weeping Willow Lane. That's out by the sports park.''

''Personally, I don't know if it's a good idea you go with me. We still need to preserve your cover,'' Dylan said. ''Maybe I should go in alone. I'll find out if he has alibis for the nights in question. Then we both can take it from there.''

''Hopefully, an alibi given by someone other than his mother,'' Celeste added.

''Exactly.''

''I still doubt we have anything to worry about. I don't think we'll ever run into each other,'' Celeste protested. ''He only goes in there early in the day, and I'm only there at night. I've heard he's not much for socialization, so I don't think he'll show up at happy hour.''

''You still haven't said too much about how it's going over there,'' Dylan commented. ''Anyone confide their deep dark secrets to the bartender yet?''

The bartender's boss kissed me as if it was the last thing he would be doing in this lifetime. He kissed me so deeply I'm still feeling it. It wasn't something she cared to divulge to her partner, no matter how good a friend he was. Especially since she was still trying to come to terms with what had happened.

Celeste had felt the tug of attraction from the first second she'd seen Luc. But she knew any kind of action on her part could hurt the investigation. Even if Luc wasn't a suspect, he was still involved in a peripheral way.

She hadn't realized that the thread of attraction ran both ways.

She barely remembered driving back to her apartment last night. She could have run every red light and not been aware. Not while her mouth still felt the imprint of his, and her body felt tight with arousal. She'd indulged in a very cold shower before she went to bed and had lain awake for hours.

"Could we turn the heater down a little?" she asked, reaching for the thermostat bar and lowering the temperature.

"Driver controls the controls," Dylan reminded, moving it back up. "It's forty degrees outside, Bradshaw. I don't intend to turn into an icicle just because you had a hot flash."

"I did not have a hot flash." She pushed it back down, then slapped his hand when he tried to adjust it. "Leave it alone!"

"Fine!" He threw his hands up, then dropped them back to the steering wheel. "What the hell is your problem? You've been acting as if you're hopping one-footed on a tightrope all morning."

"We have a rapist who doesn't leave any kind of trace evidence. Not even a finger clipping. Our only lead is a flower named Deceptive Beauty," she grumbled. "The lieutenant is on our butts."

"Because the chief is on his butt and the mayor is

on his butt,'' Dylan said. ''Yeah, it is enough to make
anyone uptight. But you usually thrive on this kind of
pressure. The more Lieu yells at you, the happier you
are. It's as if you want that challenge so you can knock
it out of the ballpark. What about the O'Brien case?
The pressure was so tough to make an arrest, even I
was ready to give up. You just said, no way, we can't
let scum like that win. A week later, we locked the
bastard up.''

''Who knows how long he would have gone on sex-
ually harassing the other teachers if you hadn't finally
talked one of them into pressing charges. After we arrested him, the others also felt brave enough to press
charges,'' she reminded him.

''Now that we've given each other a gold star, shall
we talk about how we're going to handle good ole Carl
Thatcher?'' Dylan said.

''Fine by me.'' Celeste stealthily inched the thermostat bar up a bit. Now that her thoughts had been
diverted from Luc Dante, her internal temperature had
cooled down. With luck, she could keep it that way until
she came face-to-face with the man again.

She glanced at Dylan. They'd been partners for almost two years. They had become fast friends from that
first day. Some of the other detectives and patrol officers
thought they were having an affair. They didn't bother
telling their co-workers they were wrong. That would
only create more speculation. It was better to leave it
alone.

''Here it is.'' Dylan parked in front of a cream-
colored one-story building. A redwood sign with art-
fully etched lettering proclaimed it to be Thatcher's
Trees and Flowers. He climbed out.

The rich scent of loam and plants filled their nostrils as they entered the open-air nursery.

"What do you want?"

They turned to face a woman who had to be close to six feet tall and weighed at least three hundred pounds. A moss-green cotton smock covered a light blue flow-ered top and blue pants. The name Martha was stitched in dull yellow script over a chest pocket. Her eyes were the same color as the thread.

"Mrs. Thatcher?" Dylan flashed his patented smile, meant to reassure. "I'm Detective Parker and this is Detective Bradshaw." He flipped out his ID to reveal his badge.

"I know what you are." She crossed meaty arms in front of her chest. She included both of them in her menacing glare. "I can smell a cop miles away. I just want to know what the hell you want here. We're peace-able people."

"Mrs. Thatcher, is your son, Carl, here?"

She narrowed her eyes to slits as she regarded him. "He's out making deliveries. We don't make any money unless he's doing his job, which he can't do if you interrupt his day. What do you want with him?"

"Actually, ma'am, we just want to ask both of you some questions about a few of your clients." Dylan kept smiling as if the woman wasn't looking as if she could easily toss them out one-handed.

She was as immovable as a brick wall. "Our client list is confidential."

Celeste deliberately remained in the background. She'd sensed Dylan would have a better chance with the woman if she stayed out of the conversation. She could see she was right.

"We understand that." He pulled a notebook out of

his jacket pocket and opened it. "We're just hoping you can help us clear up some things. Such as Bellmore Realty, Sierra Woods Antiques, Dante's Cafe, Kay's Fitness Center and Fieldcrest Consulting. We understand you provide plant care and fresh flowers for these businesses, correct?"

"What if we do? Is that illegal nowadays?"

"No, ma'am," he said politely, keeping his charm at a low level. It was easy to tell that charming this woman would accomplish nothing but getting them tossed off the property. "We thought that since you and your son are in those businesses on a regular basis you may have seen something that might have appeared odd to you."

Her attitude hadn't changed, but she hadn't walked away either. "Odd like what?"

"Someone not acting the way they normally would. Now, we understand you or your son delivers fresh flowers to Dante's Cafe and Bellmore Reality on almost a daily basis."

"Every morning," Mrs. Thatcher admitted. "The restaurant gets roses and Carl takes care of the plants in there. The Realtor likes a new floral arrangement for the front desk every day and they order a basket of flowers anytime they sell a house. We don't bother looking at anybody. We're just there to do a job. Either delivering the flowers or going in and taking care of plants they get from us. We don't mess in their business and they don't mess in ours."

"What about your son? Has he ever noticed anything out of the ordinary at any of the businesses he services? Maybe someone who's acted strangely or shown an interest in ordering a particular rose?"

Mrs. Thatcher snorted. "My boy doesn't gossip. It's not our nature to poke our noses where they're not wanted. He goes in, does his work like he's supposed to and leaves.''

"Do you or your son go into these businesses when they're closed? Perhaps late at night?" he asked.

"Our work is from six a.m. to six p.m."

"And your evenings? No one could say you were at any of those businesses?" Dylan delicately probed.

She stared at him as if he'd lost his mind. "Are you deaf? I just said our workday is six a.m. to six p.m. Anyone who says we've gone in when we're not supposed to is a damn liar. Tuesday and Thursday nights I'm down at the Elks Lodge playing bingo," she told him. "Monday and Wednesday and Fridays I'm out at the casino playing bingo. And my boy is with me. So who's lying about us?" she demanded.

"No one is saying anything," Dylan continued in his soothing voice. "We've just heard some things and we were hoping we could get them cleared up."

Her round face shifted as the gears in her brain worked away. "Would there be a reward if we found something out?" she asked.

"I have no word on that at this time." Dylan appeared to scribble something down in his notebook and slipped it back into his pocket. "I thank you for your time, Mrs. Thatcher." He paused as if something else came to mind. "Could I ask you a question about flowers?"

"Such as?" She still displayed suspicion.

"Roses," he said easily, lying without a qualm. "I see you have a lot of varieties around. I've heard there's a rose that's a very dark red. That it looks like there's black on the petal edges."

Mrs. Thatcher nodded. "I know the one you're talking about. In fact, you mentioned a place that gets it from us, Dante's Cafe. They like using that particular rose because it matches their décor, which has a lot of red and black."

Dylan snapped his fingers. "That's where I saw it!"

"We call it an elegant rose. People like buying anything they think is elegant," she told him, thawing a bit more. "Since it's hothouse grown, there's no fragrance, but you don't want flowers with a fragrance on your dinner table. Same with scented candles. It interferes with the food."

"So that would be a type of rose you'd give a woman?" he asked.

Mrs. Thatcher's laughter boomed outward. "Depends on what you want to tell her. Would you want to give your girlfriend a rose called Deceptive Beauty?"

Dylan grinned. "Only if the name fits."

Ten minutes later, they left the nursery with Dylan carrying several roses wrapped in green waxed paper.

"So, when's the wedding?" Celeste teased once they were back in their vehicle. "For a while, I thought she was going to ask you to go to bingo with her. From there, who knows. The woman was hot for your bod."

"Yeah, I noticed how you stood back and let me do all the talking," he grumbled.

"As far as she was concerned, I didn't exist." She settled into her seat.

"Maybe she thought the lady in basic black was my Deceptive Beauty."

Celeste smoothed the fabric of her black wool dress over her lap. "I was your basic accessory. I guess we'll have to come back when least expected so we can visit with Mrs. Thatcher's baby boy."

"Guess so. What's up, babe? You hardly ever wear

a dress on duty. Yet today you show up wearing that smart outfit.'' He raised his eyebrows.

"I thought if I looked less like a police officer and more like a woman, Mrs. Thatcher wouldn't feel intimidated. A fat lot of good that did. She was too busy looking into those sexy gray eyes of yours. I'm hoping we don't have to chase anyone down today. It's not easy running in these boots.'' She indicated her black leather high-heeled boots partially covered by the calf-length skirt of her dress. Her jacket was black leather with black wool sleeves. The dress's simple lines, with a mock turtleneck and empire waistline, suited her.

If she wanted to be honest with herself, she'd also admit a part of her hoped Luc would see her more feminine side today. After all, Sierra Vista wasn't that large a town. It was conceivable they could run into each other. She realized that Luc was taking up a good portion of her thoughts lately. Thoughts that had nothing to do with the case and everything to do with the man.

Dylan glanced at the dashboard clock. "Lunch before we go back to the station?''

"Sounds good.''

"I heard about a diner off Glen Road. Real retro.''

"Diner?'' Her mind clicked into gear.

"Yeah. They're supposed to have great burgers.''

After the performance she and Luc had given in the diner parking lot the previous night, that was the last place she wanted to be.

"How about something spicy? We could try that new Thai place over by the mall,'' she suggested. "Then we could check out some of the other florists and see if any of them carry Deceptive Beauty roses.''

Dylan looked down at the sheaf of roses he'd laid on the seat between them. In the center of the small bouquet was a deep velvety red rose with what appeared to be a hint of black feathered along the petal edges.

"She called it an elegant rose," he said. "Said that's why Dante's Cafe ordered it."

"And that it matches the décor, which it does," Celeste agreed. "The restaurant goes for a certain look with the white tablecloth, a black square cloth arranged kitty-corner over that and then the red napkins for accent. This is a place where a diner will pay serious money for a meal. And they don't serve a sliver of chicken flanked by two fancy-cut carrot curls and a swirl of sauce. The wines they serve are all award winners, many of them local. The restaurant's even been written up in area magazines."

"Exactly why no one would want to risk losing it by attacking women connected with the place." Dylan muttered under his breath when a car cut in front of him without using its turn signal. "Hey, idiot, can't you see this is an unmarked vehicle? I should hit the light and siren. Write you up," he groused at the unsuspecting driver.

"When you were a patrol officer all you talked about was making detective," she reminded him. "Now that you're a detective, you act more like a patrol officer."

"If we had the light bar and city insignia on the door, that woman would not have cut us off like that," he retorted.

"Sure, she would have. She thinks she can get away with pretty much everything."

"What makes you so sure about that?"

"She's the mayor's wife."

"We need to call the rest of the victims," Celeste said as she nibbled on pork simmered in a peanut sauce so spicy it burned all the way down her throat and brought tears to her eyes. "See if they can give us more than Janice did."

The small restaurant was overheated and redolent of exotic scents. Its popularity showed: the place was filled with hungry diners. With the tables so close together, Celeste and Dylan were forced to talk quietly so as not to be overheard. He sat to her right, their heads together as they ate their lunch and talked.

"You know what bugs me—" Dylan stabbed at his chicken and vegetables. "Two of these attacks happened on rainy nights, yet not even a speck of mud was found inside the dwellings and the rain washed away any footprints we could have found outside."

"Maybe he's your run-of-the-mill neat freak," she said. "He took off his shoes before he went inside and probably even left them outside by the door for a quick getaway. That way he wasn't heard when he got in. Look at Barbara Miller's house. It's all hardwood floors with throw rugs. No way you can be quiet when you're walking around in there. I was wearing tennis shoes that night and I could still hear my footsteps."

"And there was Marie Richardson's white carpet," Dylan added. "The only trace evidence that turned up was some fibers, but nothing we could use to pin down our guy."

Celeste thought of the clothing boutique owner's apartment that was luxurious enough to warrant a center spread in *Architectural Digest*.

"Truthfully, I couldn't imagine her ever having a lover," she said. "What man could feel comfortable in a place that looks like the inside of a freezer? The color scheme was light blue and white."

"It wouldn't be me. She'd probably shoot me the first

time I put my feet on the furniture.'' Dylan forked up some vegetables from Celeste's plate.

''Eat your own food and leave mine alone,'' she ordered, attempting to stab his hand with her fork, but he was too quick.

''You don't like these peppers anyway.''

''Not one lousy fingerprint,'' Celeste grumbled. ''Not even a partial. And nothing in the database to indicate this has been done before.''

''None of the factors we input threw up any red flags. Not the lack of trace evidence, the victims bathed and shampooed, the rose left behind on their pillows, zip.'' Dylan set down his fork.

She shook her head, frustration written on her face. ''This town isn't all that large,'' she murmured. ''It's not as if we're in San Francisco or L.A. Neighborhood Watch is a big thing around here. How many calls are received on a daily basis because someone was hanging around one of the playgrounds too much or a strange car was seen parked in a neighborhood? Yet we haven't received one neighbor's call in regard to any of these cases. I have trouble believing no one saw a thing.'' She drew random patterns on the table with her fingertip.

''Maybe someone did see something, but since it didn't appear out of place or threatening, he or she didn't think anything about it,'' he pointed out.

''So what are we talking about here? Could we be talking about someone who's seen around town so much that he's overlooked or even seems outright invisible? Like some sort of delivery person? Paper carrier, mail carrier, bottled water delivery person, package delivery person.'' Celeste ticked off on her fingers.

"Someone who leaves those advertisements on door-knobs or front gates."

"Meter readers, gardeners, cable TV repairmen, Animal Control guys," Dylan added.

She froze. She turned her head and looked him square in the eye. Her thoughts jumped into her brain at the same time as they both mouthed the words. *Police officers.* Celeste kept her gaze on Dylan's face. "I don't even want to think such a thing," she whispered fiercely.

"But you thought it at the same time I did," he whispered back. He pushed back his chair and stood up. "Let's get out of here."

Celeste grabbed her purse and followed him out of the restaurant.

"I can think of some officers who are most definitely not saints, but I can't see any of them doing such a thing," she said once they were back in their unit.

"I can't either, but we both know that doesn't mean squat." Dylan drummed his fingers against the steering wheel.

"A hunch doesn't give us anything to act on," she reminded him.

He nodded. "We could canvass neighborhoods again."

"We already asked if they saw any unknown vehicles those particular nights."

"Exactly. We used the words *strange* and *unknown.* This time we ask if they noticed a delivery truck or cable truck in the area those nights."

"Or a police car," Celeste murmured.

"We'll find a way to bring it into the conversation." He grinned. "After all, that's why they pay us the big bucks."

"Fine, but let's finish up with the florists first."

"Let's hope they're not all like Mrs. Thatcher." Dylan switched on the engine. "My patented charm can go only so far without driving women mad with desire."

"That's not the way I'd put it," she said dryly.

She was so sad. The first thing he noticed was her look of sorrow as she walked into her house. She'd been up late working the night before. She really needed to get some rest. She needed to be pampered.

She received flowers today and she tossed them into the Dumpster behind her office.

She needed someone who would truly cherish her. Give her the love she deserved.

She needed him.

Chapter 8

"Del called me last night," Jimmy announced. "He asked if he can have his job back."

The three owners of Dante's Cafe gathered every Tuesday morning for an informal breakfast meeting. They used this time to discuss any problems that might have come up in the past week. While they worked together every day, they had little chance to sit back and discuss issues unless an on-the-spot decision was required.

"No," Luc said flatly.

Jimmy turned to Paulie, who flashed him a look filled with apology.

"I have to agree with Luc on this," Paulie said softly. "We all agreed that if someone was fired for just cause we would never take them back, no matter what the circumstances."

"He said Paula had been leading him. She was making him so crazy that he wasn't thinking straight."

"The man put his hands on a woman who'd already told him to stay away from her," Luc stated in a harsh voice that brooked no argument. "To date, we have had to fire only two people. One for stealing and one for violating his parole."

"Yeah, Brett never was too smart," Jimmy said. "Trying to buy a gun from an undercover cop was sheer stupidity." He picked up his coffee cup and drank deeply, then looked around. "We get refills, don't we?" he bellowed.

The reply that came from the restaurant's kitchen was less than polite and physically impossible. The few diners in the place laughed as if they were used to the owner's irascible nature. They all looked grateful it wasn't directed toward them this time.

"If you want fancy service with some cute little waitress or starchy waiter, eat at your own place," Tank rumbled, gesturing to the coffeepot that sat on a burner. "If you want coffee and you have two legs that work, you can get it yourself."

Jimmy rumbled a few choice epithets as he slid out of the booth.

"You still scramble your eggs until they're too dry," he told the older man as he filled his coffee cup.

"That's right, insult the man who's feeding us—" Luc muttered, sliding his cup across the table when Jimmy returned with the coffeepot.

Jimmy filled Luc's and Paulie's cups, then set the pot down.

"A good way to get something disgusting next week," he added.

"I saw that write-up about your fancy place in the newspaper," Tank commented. He picked up a chair from a nearby table, flipped it around and sat down, resting his arms on the back. He cast a telling look at Luc, who pretended he didn't see it. "You three have come a long way since the day I dragged you out of that jail. I'm proud of you."

"Who would have believed street rats like us could come up with a five-star restaurant." Paulie grinned at his friends and partners.

"I think it helps that not many people know about our pasts," Luc said. "We're just known for giving people a second chance."

"So that's what you call it," Tank muttered for Luc's ears only.

"Luc?" Jimmy looked at him curiously.

"The boy was in here a couple nights ago—" Tank explained to the other two.

"I stopped for something to eat on my way home," Luc interrupted.

"What the hell was wrong with eating my food?" Jimmy pretended to take offense.

"The buffet doesn't serve cheeseburgers. Are we going to finish business?" Luc said swiftly.

"What, you got something better to do?" Jimmy kidded, sliding back across the bench seat.

"I've got some errands to run before getting over to the restaurant."

"And it's my turn to be there when Carl delivers the flowers," Paulie said. "He's also going to replace that plant that's in the corner near table seven. It's been drooping more than it should. He thinks we need a hardier plant than what's there now."

Luc kept his expression neutral as he looked out the window. Not that there was much to see when the street was gray and silver from the morning rain. "You'd think the sun had left town."

"I used to hate rainy weather," Jimmy remarked idly. "No way you could break into houses when it was too easy to leave muddy footprints behind."

"Not that many people with boats for feet either," Luc said.

"No wonder you got caught so much." Tank smacked him against the back of his head.

"Back to business!" Paulie begged between bouts of laughter. "I don't want to keep Carl waiting. His mother keeps him on a tight schedule."

Jimmy's comment about Carl Thatcher's mother was less than polite. "And I thought my old lady was bad," he said. He heaved a sigh when he saw Luc staring at him. "Okay, back to business. I'll tell Del I'm sorry, he can't come back when he gets out of jail."

"He called you from jail?" Paulie asked.

"He asked me to bail him out," Jimmy admitted. "I told him no way. Then he offered to work off the money. I told him I didn't think so. I told him he knew the rules going in. We couldn't make an exception just for him."

"But you asked us anyway." Luc shook his head in disgust. "We've worked our asses off to build up that restaurant. What if he'd done something more serious and he was linked to the restaurant? How good would that look for us?"

"Something else like what?" Paulie asked, looking at him curiously.

"Like—" Luc took a deep breath "—like that guy who's been raping women," he said in a low voice.

The other three men froze at his words.

"You think this Del you're talking about is Prince Charming?" Tank asked. He leaned forward. "Luc, do you realize what you're saying?"

"Del?" Jimmy sounded incredulous. "Come on, Luc. I read about that bastard in the papers. Could you really see Del doing all that and not leaving any evidence? Hell, there were a few times I had to remind him to wash his hands!"

"Everyone has a hidden side," Luc said.

"No way he can hide it that good," Jimmy told him.

"I'm gone," Paulie announced, getting out of the booth. "Anything else, we can finish up later today. You'll be in for the dinner shift, right?" He glanced at Luc.

Luc nodded.

"I've got a produce order coming in." Jimmy finished his coffee and stood up. "See you later," he told Luc. "And see you next Tuesday," he said to Tank. "Maybe you should get a waitress to help with the orders. Not to mention class up the joint."

"And maybe I'll show you where your suggestions go." Tank bared his teeth at him. He waited until the two men were gone before turning to Luc. "Something tells me they don't know about the little blond honey you were with or they'd be talking up a storm about her this morning. What's going on?"

Luc swallowed a sigh. He knew he'd regret not being the first to leave.

"Nothing they need to know," he muttered.

"Nothing?" Tank repeated. "You were out in my parking lot trading tonsils with the woman. No offense, boy, but she looks a little too high-tone for you, even if she did drink my coffee without flinching. Not to mention she's a cop, and you and cops don't mix."

Got it in one.

"Yes, I know," Luc said irritably. "But it's not what you think."

"I'm not so old I don't know what it looks like when two people are about ready to jump each other's bones," he rumbled as he stood up. "But you can bring her by again. She dresses up the joint and she didn't bitch about my coffee."

A tiny spot deep inside Luc warmed at Tank's praise. If the man who was called a cold-hearted son of a bitch at best liked Celeste, maybe she was someone he could trust. As long as he made sure not to trust her too much.

"I'll make sure to tell her."

That small spot was still feeling warm when Luc later walked out of the dry cleaners carrying a week's worth of laundry draped over his shoulder. A tingle started at the back of his neck and made its way down his spine.

There was a time when that feeling would have had him running for cover. This time, he tapped into his inner radar and swiveled around to face the source of that unsettling feeling.

He watched Celeste and Dylan leave a florist's shop. Their heads were together as they talked. She looked beautiful in a black dress and jacket. Her high-heeled boots added to her innate elegance. Her hair had curl in it, but her makeup was as subdued as she kept it in the bar.

Rumor has it they've hit the sheets a time or two.

There was a connection between the partners. Luc could almost see the threads between them. He still doubted whether they had been lovers, but there was a coal of unease inside him that was burning pretty hot.

If Luc didn't know better he'd swear what he felt was jealousy. He turned away before they could catch sight of him.

What he didn't know was that as he strode down the sidewalk in the opposite direction, Celeste's head snapped up as if someone had just called out her name. She unerringly turned in the direction Luc had gone. She easily found him, and kept her eyes on him until he was out of sight.

"The boss man?" Dylan asked, looking in the same direction.

"The man does have a life outside the restaurant," she said, striving to sound casual. She would have succeeded if Dylan hadn't known her so well.

"Loo-cy, what 'ave you done?" he asked in his best Ricky Ricardo accent.

Celeste threw up her hands. "Wait, I know it. I really do." She took a deep breath before proclaiming in her best dramatic voice, "Robin Williams, right?"

Dylan grabbed the door handle before she could, staying her attempt to get into the car. "I saw the look on your face, Bradshaw," he said. "Now, I know you well enough to know you wouldn't go to bed with him, but hell, who says the two of you would need a bed."

She felt the hot flash of color staining her cheeks. Staring at the car window, she said, "How heartwarming to know you have such faith in me." She pushed at him to move.

"I'm on your side, remember? Just don't set me up to be blindsided because your hormones have gone into overdrive."

"My hormones are fine, thank you very much. It's the case. All we've come up with are theories and a lead that so far has led us nowhere. Which means we're sitting around waiting for the rapist to strike again."

"Then, all we can do is hope he slips up. He might even do something stupid like leave his driver's license at the scene or fall asleep after the act." Dylan dropped his voice to the soothing tone he used with female victims. Celeste always told him he should have it patented, since it was better than any teddy bear or cup of warm milk. "Just do yourself a favor, okay? The guy you're drooling after is trouble. He was trouble from the day he was born. An incredibly heavy, sealed, juvenile record attests to that. He goes through women the way you go through your favorite chocolates. I care about you, Leste. I don't want to see you hurt."

A tiny corner of her lips lifted in a fleeting smile. She turned sideways, bumping her shoulder against his chest. "Dammit, Parker, you are way too good at this consoling bit."

"Maybe that's why the women fall asleep too soon," he joked. "Come on, we'll stop by The Chocolate Cottage on the way back to the station. I'll even spring for your candy. How does that sound?"

Her mouth immediately watered at the prospect of indulging in her favorite rich chocolate truffles. "My idea of the perfect bribe."

Dylan pulled open the car door for her. He paused when he started to close it after her. He leaned in toward her.

"Did you ever wonder about us, Bradshaw? Why we never followed through on that night?"

Celeste knew exactly what he was talking about. A night-long stakeout, too many hours cooped up in a vehicle...and during the early-morning hours, a conversation that got a little too intimate. And she knew exactly why nothing had happened. That kind of chemistry between them just wasn't there. She considered Dylan her best friend, the brother she'd never had, but she wouldn't consider taking him as her lover. She knew if they'd made love, they would have lost a friendship that was much more valuable. She'd never regretted her decision.

After meeting Luc Dante and feeling the heat between them, she understood just what that chemistry between the sexes meant. The idea of Luc Dante as a lover was disquieting and thrilling at the same time.

She hadn't given much thought to a love life. Even less to anything that could be considered long-term. She only had to look around the station to know that cops weren't a good bet in the romance department. Even then, a part of her yearned for something lasting. For the right man to love her.

She grinned. "That's easy. I'm way too much woman for you." She reached past him for the door handle and pulled it closed.

They found the station quiet when they returned to file their daily report.

"The Full Moon Pool begins today, people!" Sergeant Griffin announced, walking through the squad room. He held up a dry-erase board marked off into neat squares.

Everyone dug into their pockets and pulled out a dollar bill.

"What was the winning time last month?" one of the detectives asked.

Sergeant Griffin consulted a sheet of paper he also carried. "Barney won with 11-0-7."

"Days are shorter, moonrise will be earlier." Celeste consulted the chart. She handed the sergeant her dollar bill, then wrote her name in the square marked 10-10.

"Whatever did we do before Siegfried?" Dylan chose 9-57.

"Boring stuff like football pools." Stryker closed his eyes and stabbed at the chart with his forefinger. He wrote his name in the square his finger covered and handed the sergeant his dollar. "I'm off. Somebody stabbed a guy over at the Sierra Woods Apartments." With a wave over his shoulder, he was heading for the door.

Dylan watched him go. "That guy is way too cheerful about murder."

"More like, too cheerful about catching the murderer," Celeste corrected, walking to her desk. "It's your turn to write the report."

"But I bought you chocolate."

"I should have known you had an ulterior motive for being so generous at the shop." She logged on to the computer and typed in her password.

"Your grammar and spelling is better than mine." Dylan rummaged through his desk drawers until he pulled out a yo-yo. He was soon performing one trick after another to the amusement of the other detectives in the room.

"You keep that up, I'm calling Mrs. Thatcher and telling her you want to ask her out for dinner," she threatened silkily.

"Then I'll tell her to bring along Carl for poor little you, who's looking for a good man. And after dinner, we'll go play bingo." He easily executed an around-the-world with the yo-yo.

Celeste shook her head. "Even chocolate wouldn't be enough to get me to go along with that idea."

From his spot in the corner, Luc watched Celeste race through the kitchen. She was still wearing the dress and jacket he'd seen her in earlier in the day. She disappeared into the employee area and within minutes emerged wearing her black pants, white shirt and bow tie with her hair neatly brushed and a light rose-colored gloss on her lips. She stopped short when she saw him.

"Sorry," she apologized. "There was a fender bender on Redwood and Campbell. Getting around them wasn't easy."

"I thought you would be required to stop and assist," he murmured.

"We only have to stop if someone has been hurt." She moved toward the bar. "In between yelling at each other as to whose fault it was, both parties were on their phones, probably calling their insurance companies."

"Hey!" Flip greeted her with a big smile. The young woman stood at the bar, filling bowls with peanuts and pretzels. "I have got to tell you about this hot new guy I met at a party the other night." She glanced at Luc under the cover of her lashes. "When the big boss isn't around."

"Meaning your mom hasn't met him," he injected.

"Like she's a good judge of men." Flip made a face.

"Were you in a hurry this afternoon?" Celeste asked Luc.

He hadn't expected her to be so direct. But then, could he expect anything else with this woman?

"Excuse me?" He kept his features bland.

"You were on Main Street. You saw me. I know you did, yet you acted as if you didn't know me. You practically flew down the street. Someone would think you were running away."

Luc's jaw clenched. "I don't run away from *anything*." *Or anyone.*

Celeste didn't look convinced. She took a step closer to him. "Don't worry, Mr. Dante. You don't have to run from me if we happen to see each other on the street. I don't expect special treatment because of Sunday night.''

''We don't need to discuss this right now,'' he muttered.

''That's your problem, Dante. You don't like anyone breaking through your carefully erected defenses. Well, guess what—I've always believed in thinking outside the box. And there's no fence I can't climb.'' With that, she moved off.

Luc stood there with the sensation he'd just been run over by a blond truck.

He wasn't sure just how it had happened, but he'd swear the woman had just got the best of him. He had to leave the bar before he gave in to the suggestions racing through his mind. Foremost would have been his not wasting any time dragging Celeste over the bar— and kissing her senseless, just as he'd done the other night. Maybe if he gave in to his instincts often enough he'd be able to get her out of his system before insanity took over. Or maybe he should call one of the few women he occasionally dated. Perhaps spending the night with one of them would quell the restlessness inside him.

But deep down he knew only one woman could soothe his restless nature.

That was why he settled for leaving the bar.

''Coward,'' Celeste muttered, watching him walk away. She just wished she could figure out what was going on between them.

What he had made her feel that night still kept her sizzling inside.

She'd always told herself she didn't need a man in

her life. After this last conversation with Luc, she was pretty sure she was the last thing he wanted in his.

Celeste was grateful for a busy evening. She was kept so occupied that she didn't have a chance to think about anything other than who got what drinks.

When her break came, Celeste headed for the kitchen door and looked out. She saw a small orange light glowing at the end of the building. She grabbed two mugs of coffee and walked outside.

"This might warm you up faster than that cancer stick will." She handed him one of the mugs.

"Is this why you have such an excellent arrest record? You bug them so much they beg you to take them in?"

"I used to sing to them," she admitted. "But I had to stop when I was accused of inhumane treatment."

He glanced in her direction. "That bad, huh?"

"Dogs are known to howl." She drank her coffee to keep her teeth from chattering. "Do Flip's parents fight a lot?"

"Let's just say that if her mother says it's morning, her father argues it's evening. They're the perfect example of dysfunctional parents."

"Amazing she turned out as well as she did."

"And even with jerks like them, she's better off than if she'd been thrown into the System." Luc dropped his cigarette onto the pavement and ground it under his heel. He stared out into the parking lot.

"Did you have any fun as a kid?" she asked softly.

"Do you ever stop asking questions that aren't any of your business?"

"It's what I do."

Luc took a deep breath. ''Then try it somewhere else.''

''Why? Are you afraid I'll learn one of your secrets?''

When he turned toward her, his eyes burned with a dark fire.

''Trust me, Celeste, you don't want to go there.''

She couldn't tear her eyes away from him. The questions crowded her mind, but none crossed her lips. Without thinking, she started to lift her hand to touch his face, but her hand fell before it could reach his skin. She sensed he wouldn't welcome any type of contact at that moment.

''Didn't your mother ever tell you not to touch a hot stove, Celeste?'' He spoke softly.

''Yes,'' she whispered.

''Trying to figure me out is the very same thing. Not a good idea. Go back inside. Do what you're here to do and leave *me* alone.''

She stared at him for what felt like hours. ''I think you've been alone from the very beginning,'' she said.

Luc didn't respond or even look her way when she returned to the kitchen.

It wasn't supposed to happen that way! Why did she have to be so upset when he told her he was there to wipe the unhappiness from her eyes. Her boyfriend humiliated her! The jerk told her he needed a real woman. Since then she'd stayed in her apartment crying. He'd observed her for the past few nights. He decided tonight was perfect.

Instead, from the beginning everything went wrong. He was so scared when she grabbed her chest and cried out that she couldn't breathe. He ran. He was fright-

ened of what might happen to her, but this time he forgot to make sure that he left nothing behind. He even
stopped at a pay phone to call 911 on her behalf.

He hoped she would be all right.

He hadn't wanted to hurt her. He'd only wanted to
give her the love she deserved.

Chapter 9

"**S**orry for the early wake-up call," Dylan apologized when Celeste climbed out of her car.

Her heart sank the moment she saw the grim expression on his face.

"What happened?"

"It seems she had a heart condition," he said quietly. "When the paramedics got here, she was in cardiac arrest—911 got an anonymous call from a pay phone near a mini-mart that she needed urgent medical attention. I had one of the patrol officers go over there to question the employees to see if they got a look at anyone who used the phone tonight. The paramedics had to stabilize her before they could even take her out of her apartment. They just left for the hospital." He lowered his voice. "She didn't look good at all. An officer went with her."

Celeste looked at the apartment building. She could see lights shining from every window in one of the apartments on the first floor. Crime scene technicians walked back and forth in front of the windows. She also noticed lights on in just every other apartment in the two-story building. While some residents didn't look happy about the unexpected disturbance, others displayed open curiosity about the activity that had interrupted their sleep. She noticed some stood in their apartment doorways while others looked out their windows.

She didn't miss the variety of expressions on the women's faces, ranging from *poor her* to *thank God it wasn't me.*

The second the ringing phone had woken her at three a.m. she'd instinctively known the rapist had struck again. She had wasted no time pulling on jeans, a sweater and jacket before she headed for the address Dylan gave her.

"Have you been in there yet?" she asked now.

He shook his head. "I was waiting for you."

She took a deep breath. "Let's do it."

At the door, a patrol officer took their names and logged them in.

"Anything so far?" Celeste asked Ignacious "Iggy" Ivanovich, head of the crime scene investigation unit. Between his futile battle with an ever decreasing hairline and glasses that resembled cola bottles he was everyone's image of a scientist.

"It's just like before. He used a condom and took it with him. We're checking the tub and sink drains as always, but we've never been able to find anything there either. He got in through the front door. Definitely knows his way around a lock pick. And we have this—" He held up an evidence envelope holding a rose. "But, as always, he did leave this parting gift.

Don't worry. We'll go over this place with a microscope if need be."

"I know you will. We're heading over to the hospital to see if we can talk to the victim," she told him. "Call either me or Dylan on our cells if you get lucky and something turns up."

"Will do." He started to walk away, then stopped. "The lady's bathroom is a virtual pharmacy. Heavy-duty heart medications," he added quietly. "I'd say she was living on borrowed time."

"And now she's had the shock of being raped." She nodded grimly. "We'll need those reports ASAP."

"And you'll get them."

"We knew it was coming," Celeste muttered as she and Dylan headed to the parking lot. She glared at the onlookers. "Vultures, all of them."

"No, that's the media." They headed for his car. "All those people are just glad it wasn't them."

"Why do I have a bad feeling about this?" she asked rhetorically as Dylan sped out of the parking lot.

"Because this victim has a medical condition and her outlook isn't good."

The feeling of dread stayed with Celeste during the drive through empty streets until they reached the hospital. Her steps quickened as they walked through the automatic doors into the emergency room.

A part of Celeste's brain noted the waiting room was half-full. One little boy was curled up in a molded plastic seat, while someone who appeared to be his grandmother watched over him. A shabbily dressed man, probably homeless and looking for a warm dry spot for the night, dozed in another chair.

Dylan headed for the admitting desk.

"Hey, Teri," he greeted the clerk. "A Lori Ritter was brought in."

She nodded. "Officer Martin's back there with them. Go on back." She pushed the button to admit them.

They'd just entered when a uniformed officer approached them. He was shaking his head.

Celeste's stomach took a nosedive. "No," she whispered. She looked past him at the man dressed in wrinkled green scrubs.

"She went into cardiac arrest in the ambulance," the doctor explained. "With her weak heart, she didn't have a chance."

Dylan turned to Celeste. "Our guy just upped the stakes. Now he's not only wanted for multiple rapes, he's wanted for murder, too."

Celeste's stomach burned from too much coffee and too little food while her eyes burned from little sleep and tears she refused to shed. She sat slumped in her chair, elbow braced on the chair arm. She absently chewed on a fingernail.

Conversations flowed around her but she heard nothing. She was lost in her sorrow for a woman who may not have had quality of life, but who hadn't deserved to die the way she did.

"Here." Something was placed on the desk in front of her. "Drink it before it gets cold."

She looked at the insulated cup and smelled chicken and herbs.

"I've heard chicken noodle soup cures pretty much everything." Dylan handed her a plastic spoon.

She offered him a weak smile. "Thanks."

He perched a hip on the edge of her desk. "Leste, the woman had a weak heart that wouldn't allow her to work outside the home. She'd just gone through a bad breakup with her boyfriend that must have added to her stress. The shock of the rape was probably the last straw to her system.''

Celeste shook her head. "It doesn't matter. She shouldn't have died that way."

"No, she shouldn't have." Dylan dropped some papers on her desk. "Crime scene reports. Iggy says it's the work of our less than charming prince. Just like all the others."

"Except this time the victim died," she said tonelessly.

Celeste felt a sinking feeling in the pit of her stomach. How many rape victims had she questioned? More than one was one too many in her book. But how many had died? One. In the back of her mind she'd known the day would come when a rape victim would not survive the attack. She just hadn't expected it to happen with Prince Charming. She knew she would take some time to mourn the needless loss of life, then she would get down to work to find the bastard who had caused that loss.

"We also got a prelim report from the coroner. There was bruising along her inner thighs and on her breasts. Our guy is starting to get rough with his ladies."

She shook her head. "Not good."

"Definitely not good. I rescheduled our appointment with Barbara Miller to tomorrow morning," Dylan said. "She'd already heard the news on the radio. In the beginning, it took a lot of fast talking to get her to agree to see us again. After hearing about Lori Ritter, Barbara was more than happy to meet us. I think she's afraid he'll come back."

Celeste picked up the cup and dipped her spoon into

it. The soup warmed her stomach but couldn't reach the rest of her.

"We deal with a dark side of human nature," she murmured. "People who think nothing of hurting children, anyone weaker than them. We've told so many victims that it may take time but that they'll go on. We're not going to be able to tell Lori Ritter that."

"Death isn't a regular part of our work," Dylan said.

"Tough luck, Bradshaw." Stryker paused by her desk. He tapped the desk surface with his fingertips. His clothes were rumpled as if he'd slept in them, his sunshot hair was unruly, his square jaw unshaven and his golden-brown eyes bloodshot but warm with sympathy.

"How do you do it?" she demanded, looking up at him. "You revel in homicide cases. How do you handle all that death?" Her chin quivered. That she'd raised her voice, something she never did, that her eyes flashed fire and her body was tight as a drum attested to her inner turmoil.

"I don't let it get to me. I take it one case at a time and I don't let it eat me alive. I hate to tell you this, Goldilocks, but this isn't going to be your first death. Consider yourself lucky there hasn't been more before this one. And just realize this won't be your last." He leaned over and said something in Dylan's ear. Dylan cocked his head to listen, then nodded. Stryker moved to the rear of the room.

Celeste looked up when Sam came out of his office and gestured for her and Dylan to come into his office. He waited for them to be seated before he closed the door.

"I don't have to tell you this isn't good," he said without preamble. "It was bad enough when a woman had to worry about someone breaking in to her place and assaulting her. Now there will be panic that they'll be murdered, too."

"Which is understandable, since any woman will put herself in Lori Ritter's shoes," Dylan said. "Prelim says the shock of the rape brought on the cardiac arrest. With her heart so damaged, it was a miracle she'd survived as long as she had. Lori Ritter lived alone. She was a Web site designer. She has a sister who lives in Portland. She's flying in today to give us a formal ID of the body. I'll pick her up at the airport."

Sam looked sharply at Celeste. "Both of you will pick her up."

Dylan shifted. "Uh, Lieu, there's really no need for that."

"Both of you." He kept his eyes on Celeste. "How badly do you want this bastard, Bradshaw?"

She looked up. Her eyes were empty of all expression. She licked her lips.

"I want this guy more than I've ever wanted anything before," she said. "I want this guy so badly that I don't think I'll be sleeping until he's caught."

He studied her for several moments before nodding. "Pick up the victim's sister, transport her for the formal ID. Put her up at the Sierra Inn on our tab. And Bradshaw, tomorrow you come in here loaded for bear. Get my meaning?"

She nodded. "Loud and clear, sir. Come in ready to dig around even more." She pushed herself out of her chair.

"Are you slated to work in the bar tonight?" Dylan asked her as they walked down to the garage.

Celeste nodded.

"Maybe you should ask for the night off."

"No." Her voice was stronger. "Who knows, maybe

I'll get lucky and hear something. See something. No, I'll work.''

By evening, Celeste regretted her choice.

Lori Ritter's sister was understandably upset and angry that her sister had been pushed into dying before her time. Celeste called on every ounce of emotional reserve as she and Dylan assisted the woman in every way they could. By the time they'd left her at the hotel, Celeste was emotionally exhausted.

Flip must have sensed Celeste didn't care to talk. The normally talkative young woman kept her chatter to a minimum. Since it was a quiet night, they had little to do. Flip busied herself using the carpet sweeper over any hint of dirt and wiping off the tables almost as soon as customers left.

Luc looked in twice, but didn't come into the bar. He left her alone all evening.

''Are you okay?'' Paulie asked her when he came in for a bottle of mineral water. ''You know, if you weren't feeling well, you could have called in sick.''

''I'm not sick,'' Celeste told him, offering a smile that failed miserably. ''Maybe it's all the rain we've had lately. Too many gray days in a row. I'm sorry.''

''I know we're in the service industry, but none of us can expect to be bright and shining every day,'' he told her. ''If you don't feel well, say so. Nights like tonight don't normally bring in people who want the exotic drinks.''

''So far, the most exotic drink I've had to mix is a screwdriver,'' she replied. Her smile was a hint brighter than before.

Paulie looked around. ''Mind if I keep you company?''

''Hey, you're the boss. You don't need to ask.''

He walked around the bar and took a stool.

"So, other than too many rainy days you're doing all right?"

"Getting used to having my own room, privacy and the ability to go where I want to go when I want, yes," she said, keeping in character for Celeste Bradley, recently released felon, instead of Celeste Bradshaw, police detective. "Working here, fantastic."

His eyes were warm with understanding. "That sense of freedom is always what hits you first."

"But you, Luc and Jimmy haven't been in trouble since, when, college?"

Paulie shrugged. "We just didn't get caught," he confessed with laughter. "I think it was more self-preservation."

"Understandable." She leaned on the counter. "Could I ask you a question?"

He looked wary. "Sure, I think."

"Why do you still go by 'Paulie'?"

He chuckled. "I guess you're asking because it sounds more a kid's name, right?"

"I always thought anyone named Paulie would eventually go by Paul."

He seemed to withdraw. "My father's name was Paul and I don't like my middle name. Luc and Jimmy always called me Paulie and it stuck."

"I've heard it said that women are more prone to keep their childhood friends through adulthood than men are. Yet, the three of you have been friends for, what, forever?" She suddenly drew back. "I'm sorry, I shouldn't have asked."

"No, that's okay," he assured her. "It's not as if it's a state secret or something. We grew up in the same neighborhood. Jimmy was the bully taking lunch money from other kids. Luc was the one who could smile at a teacher and earn an A, and me—'' he took a drink ''—I was the quiet one who tried to stay out of trouble.'' He chuckled. ''And they always dragged me into it.'' He finished his drink. ''The nice thing is I can hide behind my computer in my office, which is what I prefer. Jimmy's always in his element ruling the kitchen, and Luc…'' He paused. ''Well, Luc still charms people. I guess I better get back to work.'' He smiled at her. ''Thanks for the drink.''

''Come back anytime.''

''I just might take you up on that offer.''

Celeste was relieved when she could issue a last call. And grateful the restaurant didn't stay open as late during the week as it did on the weekends. She was able to clean up early and finish her logs in short order. She was surprised when Paulie came by to escort her and Flip to their cars.

''Tomorrow will be better, you'll see,'' Flip said as they walked out to the parking lot.

Celeste patted her shoulder. ''I hope so.'' She disengaged the remote locks.

''Nice car.'' Paulie admired the sleek vehicle.

''I do love police auctions.'' She grinned.

He looked surprised. ''You're kidding!''

She shook her head. ''It was picked up in a drug bust. A friend of mine who's a mechanic goes to the auctions all the time. Of course, you're buying as is, and some aren't in the best condition or have been torn apart. He picks up cars for next to nothing, reconditions them and resells them for a tidy profit. This baby wasn't in great shape. The interior had been torn up during a search for contraband. But after some tender loving care, I had a gorgeous car for a fraction of the sale price." She opened the door.

"A little too much speed for me. I think I'll stick with my baby." He gestured toward a silver Volvo sedan.

"Jimmy was the bully. Luc was the charmer. And you were the quiet, reliable one," she said. "Good night, Paulie."

"Good night, Celeste." He closed her door after her.

When Paulie returned to the building, Luc stood in the doorway. Luc's brow furrowed.

"She's nice," Paulie explained.

"She's trouble."

"That's what you say about all women."

Luc shrugged. "And so far, I haven't been wrong." He looked at the taillights retreating in the darkness.

He hadn't missed the faint shadows under Celeste's eyes or the signs of tension around her mouth. He didn't need to be a mind reader to know what bothered her.

He'd read an account of the rape in the newspaper this morning. Then he'd heard more information about the victim on the radio. How she'd suffered a heart attack that proved fatal. Tonight's television news had shown her picture—and made his blood run cold.

He remembered her.

"I can't believe you're back for my coffee." Tank filled the mug he'd set in front of Celeste when she first sat at the counter.

"Believe it or not, I happened to be in the neighborhood," she said. "Do you think I could get an order of fries?"

"With barbecue sauce on the side."

She grinned. "You got it."

"Coming up." Tank moved back to the kitchen. Soon the sound of hot oil sizzling could be heard. "So where's Luc?"

"I don't know." She drank her coffee.

"I heard you work at his fancy place."

"I bartend there. So Luc comes in here a lot?"

"In case you haven't figured it out yet, sweetheart, I ain't an information desk. If you want to learn something about the boy, you'll have to ask him yourself." His laughter was gravelly. "But I guess you've already figured out that he doesn't like to talk about himself. What makes you think I'll tell you anything?"

"Oh, that's easy. I'm cute. People like to tell me things." Celeste studied the jukebox selector on the counter. She put in a quarter and made two selections. The raucous sounds of the Rolling Stones filled the room.

"A woman after my own heart." Tank carried out a red plastic basket filled with crisp French fries and a bowl filled with rich spicy barbecue sauce. He filled another mug with coffee. "So what's your story? Does he know you're a cop, 'cause I got to tell you, the boy just plain hates cops."

She shielded her expression. "Not in this lifetime."

Tank shook his head. "Honey, this place is loaded with cops all day long. Sometimes they'll show up at night, too. You may be pretty and have a smile that makes a man forget himself, but you still have that 'cop' look."

Celeste's curse had him laughing.

"Why are you bartending? You can't be working undercover."

"Why not?" She felt offended.

"'Cause, darlin', you suck at it," he informed her. "How many times have you worked undercover?"

"Enough, and no one has ever figured it out before."

"Probably because they were looking at the outside package." He stole a fry out of her basket and dunked it in the barbecue sauce, then bit into it. He chewed reflectively. "Not bad." He took another fry. "I'll have to pick up some of that hickory-smoke barbecue sauce. Something with more bite to it. Want a cheeseburger?"

Celeste shook her head. "Just the fries are fine, thanks."

Tank looked past her.

The tingle at the back of her neck was her first warning. She turned around.

The man standing a short distance from her was the epitome of tall, dark and dangerous. Dressed in black jeans and a black crew-necked sweater and with water droplets silvering his hair, Luc looked like a dark angel.

Memories of his mouth on hers sent a flame to the pit of her stomach. She quickly turned around and picked up another fry, almost drowning it in the spicy sauce.

"Tank." He greeted the older man as he took the stool next to Celeste. "Think I can get a chili cheeseburger?"

"Don't you ever eat at that fancy place of yours? Not that I'll turn down your money."

Luc just stared at him.

Mumbling about fancy restaurant owners who come to the wrong side of the tracks for dinner, Tank returned to the kitchen.

"Your first homicide?" Luc asked softly in a voice meant for her ears only.

Celeste nodded.

"And it got to you."

She nodded again.

"It wasn't deliberate. In his mind, he wasn't hurting her," she whispered, "except in the end he still killed her." She drowned another fry in barbecue sauce before nibbling on it.

Luc reached across her and picked up a fry.

"What brought you here?" he asked.

"I was hungry for world-class fries and Tank definitely makes world-class fries."

"Damn straight, sweetheart." Tank didn't mind letting them know he was unashamedly eavesdropping on their conversation. He ignored Luc's frown.

Luc turned back to Celeste. "He knows?"

"He guessed." She moved the basket to sit between them.

"If you were having problems because of last night you could have called in sick," Luc told her.

"No, I couldn't. That would have meant I was running, and I won't do that." Suddenly feeling very tired, she pushed her hair away from her forehead and covered her face with her hands. "She never had a chance." Her words were muffled by her hands. "She worked from home because of her frail health. She had a boyfriend, and tonight her sister is grieving because her baby sister won't be visiting for Christmas."

Luc glanced up when Tank set a plate in front of him. He flicked the bun off his burger and glanced up at Tank, then snapped his glance back down to the burger sans chili. Tank stared at him, glanced at Celeste, then back to Luc.

"We're out of chili," he said flatly.

With a sigh, Luc picked up the cheeseburger and bit into it. Tank returned to the kitchen.

"I had seen her at the restaurant," he said in a low voice.

Celeste turned her head. "What?"

Luc nodded. "The woman. I saw her picture on the news late today and I remember her being at the restaurant a few times," he reluctantly admitted. "The reason I remember her is that she and her boyfriend celebrated her birthday there a couple weeks ago."

"So there could be a connection."

"Or nothing more than a coincidence," Luc argued, but he didn't sound convinced.

They finished their food in silence while Tank cleaned the kitchen.

Luc studied the jukebox selector. Then he pulled out a quarter, slipped it in the slot and punched in his choices. The mellow sounds of the Righteous Brothers flowed out of the speakers. He slid off the stool and held out his hand.

"Dance with me," he invited in a husky voice that sounded as if he wanted to invite her to do more than just dance.

She hesitated.

"Give the boy a break and dance with him," Tank boomed. "He never got to go to his prom."

"You're not helping," Luc growled, keeping his dark gaze on Celeste's face.

Celeste put her hand in his and slid off her stool. When she stepped closer, he enfolded her in his arms so that her cheek was nestled against the soft wool of his sweater. She fit perfectly in the curve between his shoulder and neck. She slid her arms up and around his neck. She inhaled the woodsy scent of his skin that was mixed with a faint hint of tobacco and just plain Luc. They moved together as one as they swayed across the ancient linoleum. When the song finished, another immediately came on. They had no idea that Tank fed the jukebox several quarters as they continued dancing to music appealing to lovers, or that he turned off most of the lights to add to the atmosphere.

If Celeste had to describe the moment, she would have said she felt comforted. Even safe. She closed her eyes and allowed herself to flow with the music and just plain forget the past twelve hours. There would be time tomorrow to remember the sorrow she was dealing with.

When the music eventually stopped, their feet still moved together for several moments.

"As much as I've enjoyed the show, boys and girls, this old man needs his ugly rest." Tank laughed at his own joke. He shook his head when Celeste pulled out her wallet. "No charge."

She narrowed her eyes. "No bribing the fuzz." She dropped the bills on the counter.

Still not saying a word, Luc picked up Celeste's jacket and helped her into it. They walked outside to her car.

"What will you do now?" he asked, finally breaking the silence between them and bringing the present screaming back into their lives.

"Dylan and I are seeing one of the first victims tomorrow," she replied. "Sometimes, distance allows them to remember things they might not have thought of before. We're hoping we'll be able to talk to all of them. After last night—" she choked the last two words "—they might be more willing. It's never easy for them to begin with. Hearing that someone has died makes it even harder to get past the trauma."

"Why do you do this?" he asked. "Why aren't you married to some up-and-comer with your two-point-five children and a pedigreed Golden retriever, and spending your weekends at the Sierra Vista Country Club?''

"Actually, I am a member of the country club because of my parents, but most men in my parents' social circle aren't too comfortable dating a woman who's armed. And I do it just because." She held up her hand. "It's not something I can talk about just now, so please don't ask any more. Unless you're willing to trade old war stories." She wasn't surprised to see the withdrawal in his eyes. "I thought so." She reached for the door handle, but he beat her to it.

"My past wasn't as normal as yours. It didn't consist of private schools and all the right friends and parties," Luc said harshly. "I've lied, cheated, stolen. I knew every cop and they knew me. You were probably voted Most Likely to Succeed. I was voted Most Likely to End Up in Prison. Believe me when I say I am literally a son of a bitch.''

Celeste tipped her head back so she could look into his eyes. She wondered if he preferred his black wardrobe because he didn't believe he could have any color in his life.

"But you proved them wrong," she said.

"Only because that wasn't how I wanted to end up. I wasn't going to end up like other kids I ran with. Most of whom are either dead or in prison.''

"Which must have made your mother happy."

The dark fury that crossed his features would have frightened a lesser woman. Even Celeste pulled back a little.

"You don't want to know." He leaned forward to press his mouth roughly against hers, then just as quickly withdrew.

"No!" Celeste snarled, grabbing hold of his sweater

front and pulling his face back down to hers. Her mouth was hot silk as she kissed him with a wildness that was unlike her. Her hands dove under his sweater, seeking the heat of his body to warm her as she moved against him. This time she was the one to pull back. Her silvery-green eyes glittered. "For the first time in almost twenty-four hours I am *feeling*," she told him. "I have felt numb since I heard Lori Ritter was dead. Now, instead of that numbness, I feel alive again. And whether you like it or not, it's because of *you*."

Luc's face twisted in an agony that came from the soul.

"It's the ups and downs of the day, nothing more," he said coldly. "Go home, go to sleep, and when you wake up you'll be glad I didn't take you to bed with me." He gently pried her fingers from his sweater and walked to his car.

A dazed Celeste watched him climb into his car and drive off with a squeal of tires. The adrenaline that had coursed through her when they kissed was slowly dissipating, leaving her feeling unsettled and unfulfilled.

"If this keeps up, Tank will start charging admission for the show," she murmured.

The wheels inside her head started turning. Her curiosity about Luc Dante was growing and there was one person she had in mind to help her.

"Just because he doesn't want to talk about his past doesn't mean I can't find someone who *will* talk about it."

"What else have you got? Uh-huh. Yeah." Stryker's pen raced across the paper. He was slouched back in his chair with his booted feet resting on the desktop. A yellow legal pad was propped on his flat stomach.

"When did he get out?" An insulated tall cup of what smelled like fresh brewed coffee seemed to float in front of his eyes. He glanced up. "Okay, thanks. Gotta go," he said into the receiver before he hung up.

"What brings you down here to the depths of hell?" He took the cup before it was snatched from his sight. He opened the lid and inhaled the aroma, then sipped the coffee. "And why the bribe?"

Celeste used her foot to push his chair over as she hitched herself up onto his desk. "Who says it's a bribe?" she asked archly.

Stryker looked around the empty corner of the squad room that comprised the homicide department. The only desk occupied just then was his. Just the way he liked it.

"Come on, Goldilocks, this isn't your style. One thing I've always admired about you is your directness. Don't BS a champion BSer, okay?" He drank his coffee.

"Okay." She took a deep breath. "I want to know about Luc Dante."

Stryker stared at her for several moments. "One part owner of popular restaurant, Dante's Cafe. Thirty-five, single, considered a hot property among the female sex. He's heterosexual, which *really* makes him a prime catch. He lives alone. Pays his bills on time, has a nice apartment, no pets. Anything else?"

"You knew him when you were kids." It was a guess on her part, but deep inside, she knew she was right. His reply confirmed her hunch.

"And?"

"What was he like then?"

"Now that's the direct Goldilocks I know." Stryker nodded his approval. "We were all hell-raisers. Luc went to college, I went into the army. Bad boys made good. End of story.''

"No!" She grew frustrated. "What was he like as a person? Why does the mention of his mother make him so angry?"

He blew out a low whistle. "You asked him about his mother? Man, you are one brave lady."

"What about her?" Celeste demanded. "You know something, don't you."

He shook his head. "Not a good subject, Goldilocks. Give the guy a break and leave it alone. Better yet, leave him alone, too." His voice softened. "Before it goes too far. You're a good cop, but honey, guys like us are bad news for women like you." He raised his cup. "Thanks for the coffee. Now be a good girl, go home and get some sleep. You've got a rapist to catch."

Celeste shook her head.

Stryker easily read the emotions crossing her face. "Oh, man," he groaned. "You're hooked on the guy. It's the case that's doing it to you. Once this case is over you'll go on with your perfect life and you'll be grateful you didn't make any mistakes like sleeping with the guy."

She acted coy. "Who says I haven't?"

Stryker shot her a telling look. "Honey, trust me, if you'd been between the sheets with Luc, I'd know it. You don't want that." His voice softened a fraction. "You'd only end up hurt. Listen to Uncle Jared. Luc won't thank you for looking into his past. Do your job. If you want to obsess, obsess about your case. Not a man who isn't worth your time."

Celeste shook her head. "Then I'd say this time good ole Uncle Jared is wrong. And I think that's part of the problem with Luc. No one ever thought he was worth their time—and he most definitely is.''

He didn't bother putting on any lights when he got home. He knew every inch of the place. Besides, he was blessed with excellent night vision.

He prided himself at never drinking alcohol at work. Home was a different matter.

He splashed whiskey in a glass and downed the contents in one gulp. It burned a fiery trail down his throat and settled warmly in his stomach. A second drink soon followed.

Carrying a glass that was filled with yet a third drink, Luc walked into the family room and settled in a chair. He stretched his legs out in front of him and morosely stared at the window.

It had started to rain again. He watched rivulets trail down the glass, glittering from the streetlight just outside the building. A faint hum indicated the furnace had just kicked in. Warm air blew gently against the back of his neck.

He had everything he hadn't had as a kid. He owned a nice apartment with even nicer furniture. He put on quality clothing every day. Ate good food so he never grew hungry. He had money in the bank so he never had to worry from day to day. If he wanted company there were women who would be only too happy to help him keep his bleak loneliness at bay.

So why was he sitting here alone in the dark thinking about a blond detective whose smile lit up his world? Who kissed him as if there were no tomorrow? With her in his arms, he knew he would die a happy man.

The whole situation was ridiculous. The last thing he needed in his life was a woman who came with a practically blue-blooded pedigree, while he had no idea who his father was. She was a woman who spelled *long-term* in big block letters. Celeste Bradshaw wasn't dangerous because she carried a gun. She was dangerous because she touched something that he'd hidden deep inside him.

His peace of mind was gone because of her. He didn't sleep well, because sleeping meant dreaming about her. Wishing she was lying in his bed. Wishing she was touching him the way he wanted to touch her. Wishing for a future he knew he could never have.

He feared if she remained working undercover at Dante's Cafe for too much longer, she would prove even more dangerous to his soul than she already was to his senses.

She hadn't backed down when he'd told her he was a son of a bitch. But then, she had no idea just how accurate his statement was.

Chapter 10

Celeste entered the station with the determination of a woman on a mission, and woe to anyone who dared stop her. As she walked in, Stryker was on his way out. He glanced at her and shook his head.

"Did anything I said last night sink in?" he asked.

"Yes. I now know bribing you with coffee does me absolutely no good." She slapped the door with the flat of her hand and sailed on past him.

"Maybe the two of you do deserve each other," he called after her. "You're both too stubborn to listen to the voice of reason."

"Tell you what, when the voice of reason shows up, I'll listen," she tossed over her shoulder.

Dylan was talking on the phone when Celeste dropped into her desk chair. He glanced up and nodded at her.

"That was an extremely expensive cactus," he said. "What you did could have killed it." He listened. "I was only told to pay you one hundred dollars a month alimony. It was never stated just how that payment was to be made. I've gotta go.'' He hung up.

''They say *women* never get off the phone, yet every time I come in here, I find a guy on the phone, not a woman,'' Celeste said, leafing through her messages.

''Your mother called twice,'' Dylan said. ''She said you're due for the family dinner and you can even bring me along. She's afraid I'm not eating right. She also asked if you're making sure your gun isn't loaded when you go out. I explained to her that it's loaded but you're very careful with it. You know, I love Marina, but you need to sit her down and explain to her that the way we work isn't like the Humphrey Bogart and Edward G. Robinson movies on cable.''

She glanced at the jelly doughnut on his desk. ''Good thing she doesn't have video phone or she'd be lecturing you on processed sugar, saturated fats and high cholesterol. As for her take on cops, she's a big fan of *NYPD Blue* and *Law & Order*.'' She tossed her messages on her desk. ''What time is Barbara Miller expecting us?''

''Eleven. We're meeting her at her studio. I also called Lauren Davis since her shop is in the neighborhood. She was really hesitant about us coming by. She's not too eager to see us, so I had to do some persuading. She's pretty upset after hearing about Lori Ritter. She's afraid if she talks to us again, he might come back and kill her. I explained that Lori's death was due to her aggravated medical condition. That he didn't purposely kill her, even if he's responsible for her death. That's why I pushed for a meeting today. I was afraid she'd back out if she has too much time to think about it.''

''I don't blame her. If it were me, I'd be scared, too,'' she admitted. ''It's bad enough to worry about being attacked in your home, but to think you could die as a result is frightening. This guy hasn't been violent and that's a plus. Now the crimes have been taken to a whole new level. You need to think about this from her perspective. Get in touch with your feminine side," she advised.

"Since you'd be much better at it, I'll leave that up to you."

Celeste picked up one of the message slips. "They set a court date on the Grant case?" She mentioned a child-abuse case she and Dylan had investigated. Fire-fighters going out to a house fire had discovered an eight-year-old girl and ten-year-old boy locked in a bed-room while their parents were at work.

Dylan nodded. "D.A.'s office says the kids were placed in their maternal grandparents' custody and go-ing to weekly counseling."

She nodded. "At least something good will come out of it. Nothing else on the Ritter apartment?"

Dylan shook his head. "So far, nothing new."

Celeste looked around. "Where's the boss?"

"Lieu's in court. Some old case of his is up for ap-peal." Dylan picked up three pink rubber balls and be-gan juggling. "He was stomping around here earlier. Asked where you were."

Celeste felt instant guilt. She never overslept, but af-ter her late-night visit to the station, then keeping watch out her bedroom window for a few hours after she re-turned to her apartment, she hadn't gotten much sleep. When she got in, she'd glanced out the window and noticed a shadow across the street again. It was eerily similar to the one she'd seen before. She'd stayed up looking out the window until she dozed off. When she awoke later, she found the shadowy figure gone. She'd gone to bed after that, sure she wouldn't be able to fall asleep, but she was so exhausted that she fell asleep almost immediately and slept through her alarm. She'd raced through getting ready and skipped breakfast so she wouldn't be late getting into the station. At the moment she craved coffee more than life itself.

"No one else is as lucky with the Full Moon Pool as you are, Bradshaw," one of the detectives called out. "You splitting the winnings with Siegfried?"

"If I did, Langdon, he'd come in here wearing clothes," she told him. "On behalf of the women's shelter I'd like to thank all of you for choosing the wrong time."

"What would we do without ole Siegfried for entertainment?" Dylan mused.

"Look for someone else who's convinced they were bitten by a werewolf?"

"I didn't realize our esteemed police department hunted down werewolves, too."

Celeste spun around so fast she almost fell out of her chair.

"What are you doing here?"

Luc looked devastating in black jeans and a black polo shirt topped by a black jacket. What also caught her attention were the two coffee cups he carried.

"I come bearing gifts." He set one in front of her. "I've noticed cops live on coffee, so this seemed to be the appropriate admission price." He offered her the smile filled with charm she'd seen many times, except now there was something in his eyes that she had only seen twice before. The two times he'd kissed her.

Maybe there was hope for the man after all.

"Definitely." She grasped the cup almost lovingly.

He perched his hip on the edge of her desk. "And why are you hunting werewolves?"

"Just one. Siegfried," she replied. "He's become a monthly fixture."

"About two years ago, Siegfried was bitten by a dog. He was convinced it was a werewolf," Dylan explained. "Since then, he comes in here every month, the first night of the full moon, insisting he needs to be caged. Since he comes in stark naked, we accommodate his request. In the morning, someone drives him home."

"I'm surprised you don't call in the psychiatrists," Luc said.

"He's actually harmless," Celeste explained. "I think he's a lonely guy looking for attention. And he only howls a couple times during the night. We started up a pool on the time he'll show up. It's a dollar a guess."

"Bradshaw's won the past few months," Dylan said. "But she does it for good," he intoned. "She gives the money to the women's shelter. Any month she doesn't win, she guilts the winner into donating the winnings."

"That's why I'm not invited to the weekly poker games." She finished her coffee, then fastened her greedy gaze on Luc's cup. He handed it to her. She smiled her thanks. "Once again, what are you doing here?"

"What can you tell me about this case?"

"Nothing," Dylan said, looking from one to the other.

"You've got to understand we can't tell you any details of the case," Celeste told him. She could feel the tightening in her stomach. After spending most of the night thinking about him, seeing the man in the flesh was almost more than she could handle. Judging from Dylan's narrowed gaze, he was reading her mind.

"Even though it involves my restaurant?"

"Especially because it could involve it," she said softly. She shot Dylan a warning look that he blithely ignored. She stood up and grasped Luc's arm, pulling him off balance. "Let me walk you to your car." She pushed and prodded him toward the door.

"I bring you coffee and you show me the door," he protested.

She didn't say a word until they reached the parking lot, and ignored the curious looks directed their way.

"You act like the coldest-hearted bastard in the state last night, then you show up this morning with coffee and smiles." She kept her voice low, vibrating with fury, while her lips were stretched in a smile that equaled his in charm. "Did you think you could give me caffeine and I'd spill details? I don't think so!"

Luc looked over her head and off into the distance.

"I remembered Lori Ritter," he murmured. "She had a special diet. We always accommodated special food needs, but she was embarrassed at asking for no butter or cream sauces. She had a very sweet nature. She shouldn't have died that way."

"No one should die that way, Luc," Celeste said.

"I want to do something, anything, but I feel powerless," he admitted.

Celeste hadn't expected his stark admission. She thought for a moment. "I'll see what I can do and let you know tonight."

His gaze roamed over her. A corner of his mouth curved upward. "Funny, you don't dress like a cop."

She looked down at her black tailored pants topped with a fine wool aquamarine turtleneck top, and matching wool and silk sweater jacket with an asymmetrical collar.

"This is Sierra Vista not San Francisco," she said dryly. "The mayor doesn't like the cops looking like cops. We're supposed to blend into the background."

"Honey, I don't think, even in uniform, that you blend in anywhere."

"Does anyone at the cafe know what I really do?"

He nodded. "I concede. You can blend when you want to."

She felt the hum of danger in her blood. She toyed with the idea of tweaking the dragon's tail, so to speak.

"So I can do anything I want?" she asked softly, moving closer to him. She inhaled the clean scent of soap and man.

"Bradshaw, phone for you!" Dylan stood just inside the front door.

Celeste waved over her head to show she heard him.

"I will see what I can do," she promised, backing away.

"Tell me something. Why didn't you and Parker ever become an item?"

"Who says we haven't?"

"I've seen the two of you together," he stated, as if that said it all.

She inclined her head to concede his point. "He never made my blood sing," she said simply.

Luc looked away, then swung his gaze back to her. "What happens when you're with me?"

Celeste's smile was pure sunshine. "Let's just say when I'm around you my blood belts out the *Hallelujah Chorus*." She blew him a kiss. "Now I have to go before Parker gets cranky."

Celeste ran back toward the building, aware of Luc's dark gaze on her every step of the way.

"Seems you called a Harry Kramer in Juvenile?" Dylan commented.

She mentally cursed. "That's who's on the phone?"

"Yep. Now, why would you be calling a retired juvenile officer?"

Celeste continued walking to her desk. She picked up her phone and punched in the button that blinked. "Detective Bradshaw," she said crisply.

"Bradshaw, this is Kramer. Now, why the hell are you disturbing my retirement to ask me about that old son of a bitch Luc Dante?"

I am a son of a bitch.

"You realize his juvenile record's sealed," the man went on. "Whatever he did as a kid can't be brought up again."

She pulled her thoughts back. "Yes, I realize that. Actually, I'm only trying to find out about the man himself. Not his record." She could hear a faint wheeze on the line.

"Why?"

She glared at Dylan, who was openly listening in on the conversation. He merely settled back in his chair, lacing his fingers over his flat stomach.

"Some things have come up in a case I'm investigating in which Mr. Dante is involved. Not as a suspect, but as a consultant. I'm trying to get a handle on the man himself and I thought finding out something about his past would help," she said. "Naturally, with his juvenile record sealed, my best bet is to speak to anyone who dealt with him back then. I understand you worked that division at the time."

Harry Kramer barked out a laugh. "Okay, honey, in

a nutshell, Luc Dante was the kid from hell who knew how to charm a penny out of a miser. I wouldn't have given you a plugged nickel for that little bastard. I kept telling him he'd end up dead or in prison. There's more than one unsolved crime from years ago that I'm convinced he was behind. Now the mayor's calling him by name and acting as if Dante grew up normal. Trust me, honey, he didn't. He was no good then and he's no good now, no matter how much he pretends to be a so-called businessman. Him and his friends are nothing more than street rats all grown up. I'd still like to see them in a cell where they belong."

She felt a chill inside. If this was what Luc had heard as a boy, no wonder he didn't like cops.

"As I said, he's not a suspect in this case. In fact, he's been instrumental in assisting us," she explained.

"The only one he assists is his own self," he said flatly. "I get the picture now. Honey, you're not the first broad he's humped and dumped and you won't be the last. Do yourself a favor and move on." He hung up.

"Harry Kramer worked Juvie for almost thirty years. A real hard-ass, too." Dylan leaned toward her to whisper, "So why are you calling him about Luc Dante?"

"Maybe I want to know about the man we're working with," she replied. She glanced at her watch. It was still much too early to go to see Barbara Miller. "He told me that Lori Ritter had been at the restaurant not all that long before the rape."

Dylan pushed aside papers until he found his notebook. "Did he give an exact date when she was there?"

"He didn't say." Celeste paused. "He wants to be involved with the case."

Dylan's head whipped back and forth. "No, no, no.

There is no way we can allow that. You didn't tell him yes, did you?''

"Give me credit, Parker," she snapped.

"I'm beginning to wonder. He shows up with coffee for you. You're trying to find out about his juvenile record. Come on, Leste, what's going on?" he asked.

"What do you think is going on? I'm trying to solve a case that's barely given us a break!" she snapped. The last thing she wanted was for him to figure out her feelings for Luc. "If you'd concentrate more on your work and less on interrogating me, maybe we'd get somewhere."

Dylan reared back. "Fine." He returned to his desk and dropped into the chair.

Celeste felt guilt tease the back of her mind, but she didn't voice an apology for almost taking his head off. Instead, she returned to leafing through her notebook to review their last interview with Barbara Miller. She remembered the woman was a landscape artist who worked in oils and that she owned a successful gallery that featured local artists. She tapped her pen against the edge of the desk. "One more thing. Every victim has been fairly successful in her respective field. None has a husband who works nights. In fact, none is married. They've all been single."

"Which means he's a rapist with a skewed moral code. He doesn't go after married women. It's already been said the roses left on the pillow are his way of romancing them." He began juggling his balls again, this time four of them. Then he started tossing them one by one to Celeste, who tossed them back to him.

"So does he need to target single working women to feel superior in some way or because he feels they're his equal?" she mused.

"Or because he thinks they need romance."

"But they all had men in their lives."

"Janice Bowen and her fiancé broke up," Dylan said.
The gears in Celeste's brain started clicking away.
"That didn't happen until after the rape, but for all we
know they might have been having problems before
then. And Lori and her boyfriend had recently broken
up."

They stared at each other as if a silent conversation
flowed between them.

"What about the others?" She rapidly skimmed her
notes. "Did you write anything down about their love
lives?"

"Marie Richardson had a boyfriend, but they weren't
getting along," Dylan added. "Nothing on Barbara Miller. You?"

Celeste shook her head. "Zip. We'll have to ask
her." She reached into her desk drawer and withdrew
a chocolate truffle. She nibbled on the sweet as she
continued studying her notes.

"How can you eat that so early in the day?"

"I didn't have time for breakfast," she said defen-
sively. "Besides, it's like having a chocolate doughnut."

"Not even close. And you make fun of my eating
habits."

"Chocolate is like a basic black dress. It goes with
anything," she said loftily, finishing her candy. "I think
we'll need to not only ask Barbara if there's a man in
her life, but if there's also been problems lately with
her love life."

"Sounds like a plan to me. I think it should be our
number one question," Dylan said.

Celeste nodded. "It's at the top of my list. But first

you're going to have to feed me. I didn't have time for breakfast this morning.''

Dylan snapped his notebook shut as he stood up. ''We'll leave now so we can hit a fast-food restaurant on the way. I don't want you embarrassing me with a growling stomach.''

Later, pacified with a sausage and biscuit, a food choice that would have horrified her mother, Celeste felt better. She and Dylan parked in the small side lot next to the Miller Gallery. They paused at the bay window that displayed two paintings.

Dylan studied one canvas that looked like slashes of red, black, yellow and bright blue. ''Is it me or does that picture make you feel incredibly depressed?'' he asked.

Celeste did her own perusing. ''There's an awful lot of black paint splashed across it.''

''Your professional take?''

She shrugged. ''This isn't a Rorschach test.'' She noticed movement inside the gallery. ''She sees us. We better go inside.'' With Dylan on her heels, she pushed open the door.

''Barbara.'' With a warm smile on her lips, Celeste walked up to the woman with her hand stretched out. ''How are you doing?''

Celeste knew Barbara Miller was in her late forties, but she took great care of her looks, shaving a good ten years off her age. She wore a black knit tunic top and slim-cut pants, her only accent a bold silver belt that hung loosely on her hips. Silvery-blond hair was pulled back in a braid. The shadows under her eyes were minimized with concealer and her pale features were highlighted with a bare hint of blush. It was her eyes that struck Celeste the most.

This was a woman who was very afraid.

"Why haven't you caught him yet?"

Celeste remembered the woman was someone used to being in control. The sad thing was, in the space of a few hours, Barbara had lost that sense of control, leaving her feeling vulnerable.

Curtains now covered windows that looked out over the rear of the building. An extra dead bolt guarded the rear door and a new security alarm keypad had appeared on the wall by the door. Celeste wondered if it had been done since news of Lori Ritter's death hit the papers.

"I should have done it long ago," Barbara said, noticing the direction of Celeste's gaze. She threaded her fingers together, then released them. "Would you like some coffee?"

Sensing the woman needed to keep busy, Celeste and Dylan accepted her offer and followed her to the rear of the building.

"Erin, we'll be back in my office," she called out to her assistant, a young woman in her twenties. "If anyone calls, just take a message. I don't want to be disturbed."

The decor of Barbara's office depicted the woman before her life changed. Brightly colored pillows splashed color across the oatmeal-colored fabric chairs and couch.

Celeste accepted the coffee as she seated herself on the couch beside Dylan. Barbara chose a chair to Celeste's left.

"I realize this is difficult for you," she said.

"Difficult?" Barbara laughed without humor. "They tell you to go forward. It's not easy to do when you have constant reminders. And now women are dying."

"Yes, now women are dying," Celeste said firmly.

"Detective Parker and I are doing everything possible to track this person down before anyone else is hurt. As you know, this man hasn't left any evidence that will help us find him. I know you don't want to relive that night, but we're hoping if you think about it, you might remember something. Perhaps something happened when you were first awakened, or maybe you remember something about his voice, or maybe even something else that you may have dismissed before?"

Barbara closed her eyes and shuddered. She shook her head. "I can't," she whispered. "I just can't. The bastard talked to me as if he were my lover, and when he talked, he whispered. There was no accent, no way of saying words that gave a hint. When he was finished, he bathed me as if I were some precious possession of his!" Her face twisted with revulsion. "He acted as if we were a couple."

"I once read an article about you, where you said you paint from your soul," Dylan said.

"How would I paint him?" she asked, easily guessing what was coming.

He nodded.

She sat very still, except for her hands, which restlessly picked at the nap of her pants.

"Orange," she said finally.

"Orange?" Celeste and Dylan looked at each other.

Barbara nodded. "Not the color, the scent. When I paint, I paint using all my scents. I keep bowls of potpourri around or I burn candles. He wore gloves, but I could smell orange on his skin, on his arms. Maybe an orange-scented soap. Does that help?"

"It definitely could," Celeste agreed. "Does anything else come to mind?"

Barbara shook her head. It was clear she didn't want to try any longer.

"We thank you for talking to us," Celeste said, sensing the interview was over. "If anything else occurs to you, please call us."

"As much as I want this disgusting animal caught, the last thing I want is to remember more," Barbara said. "But now I understand why I can no longer abide orange juice."

"Well, that last five minutes reminded me of my last date," Dylan muttered as they walked back to their vehicle.

"Her practically pushing us out the door?"

"That—and the paints, except she wanted to use finger paints."

She sighed. "Okay, I'll bite. She wanted to paint your picture using finger paints?"

Dylan feigned impatience. "No, she wanted to paint *me* with her finger paints."

"If anyone heard us, they'd think we don't care," she said.

"Yeah, well, if we didn't make jokes, we'd be fitted for those cute little white jackets with all the buckles," he told her. "You're the one with the psych degree. You'd know that better than most."

"I do." She grimaced as raindrops hit her face. "I'm ready for some dry weather!"

"Look on the bright side. We have another lead."

"Let's see if anyone else mentions orange-scented skin."

Dylan glanced back at the building. "She's scared as hell."

Celeste nodded. ''Yes, she is, and as a result she's made herself a prisoner in her own territory. I bet her house is just as secure as the gallery. The sad thing is, she won't be free until she's ready to free herself.''

Chapter 11

Celeste didn't see Luc when she walked into the restaurant that evening, but she knew he was there. All she had to do was feel that flutter inside her stomach and tingle along her nape.

She hadn't bothered telling Stryker she wasn't about to pursue Luc. That she kept private. She'd allowed few men into her life. She didn't feel the need to have one around full-time and she hadn't met anyone who could handle her job. She'd come home from more than one date convinced she was better off with her fish.

Since the evening was slow, she and Flip decided to use their free time to rearrange the tables.

"What are you doing?" Luc scowled at them as he walked in.

"It looks nicer this way," Celeste explained, pushing a chair back up against a table.

He looked around. *"Feng shui?"*

Flip giggled.

"More like easier to navigate around the tables whether you're entering from the dining room or the entryway," Celeste said.

Luc looked around and could see that the subtle changes she and Flip had made with the tables accomplished exactly what she'd said.

"Just no lace curtains on the windows," he murmured as he walked around the bar and pulled out two bottles of sparkling water. He set them on the bar along with two ice-filled glasses. He poured the water into the glasses and added a twist of lime and a straw to each. He glanced at Flip. "Isn't it time for your break?"

"Uh, no—oh." She looked from one to the other. "Yes." She scurried out of the room.

"It didn't take you long to clear the room," said Celeste.

"It's a gift." He carried the two glasses over to one of the tables and set them down. "Have a drink."

She took the chair next to him. "It's not time for my break."

"Boss's prerogative." He glanced at the straw he'd put in the glass, then discarded it. "Never did like them. Guess I put it in out of habit. I worked as a bartender my junior year in college."

"Hear any good stories?" She sipped her drink.

"There was Warren, who came in every night to lament about Sheila after she dumped him for Tony. I learned a lot more about Sheila than I ever wanted to know," he recalled. "Including her habit of chewing bubble gum during sex."

"That must have been sticky," Celeste said deadpan.

"Only when she blew bubbles." He waited a beat. "I still want to help out with your case."

She nodded. "I know."

He must have read the expression on her face. "And your partner disagrees."

"Civilians aren't allowed to get involved—for many reasons. Liability is just one of them."

"Then, spend some time with me tomorrow. Pick my brain about the people who work here, my recollections of the victims," he suggested. "I promise to be good, so your partner won't have to come along."

"Gee, Luc, you're making it sound like a date," she laughed.

"Spend tomorrow with me," he said again, his expression softening.

Celeste could think of a hundred reasons why she shouldn't spend time with him.

"We're in the midst of a difficult case," she said slowly. "It's not a good time for me to take a day off."

"Even to interview someone who might be able to help with the investigation?" he pointed out. "I would think your superiors would be happy that you have the chance to talk to an outside source."

"Outside source," Celeste murmured. The idea of spending the day with Luc was tempting. She might even get lucky and...*no!* She gave her brain a smack for veering off the straight and narrow. She meant she might get lucky and indulge her curiosity about Luc, the man. One look into those bottomless deep blue eyes was enough to send any woman thinking about things that were better off unthought.

That was her story and she was sticking to it.

"Maybe you can come up with something we haven't thought of," she conceded.

"I'll pick you up at nine. If what you gave me was your real address."

"It's where I'm presently living." She finished her

drink and stood up. ''Time to get back to work before the boss catches me slacking off,'' she confided with a whisper. She picked up his glass.

Celeste was aware of Luc's gaze as she walked back to the bar.

She considered her meeting with Luc tomorrow to be work, but there was a part of her that wondered if it wasn't really a date.

He followed her to make sure she got home safely. That was why he stayed out here and watched as her apartment lights went on one by one. It had started raining again an hour ago, but he didn't notice the rain or cold weather. Watching over her gave him a warm feeling. And when the time came, he'd show her just how much she meant to him. He would give her everything she deserved and more.

Bare skin moved against bare skin. Parted lips as soft as silk slid across his chest. The words whispered were erotic, praising him. Her hands were equally magical as they trailed downward until they found the spot he ached for her to touch. He arched up, alternately cursing her and giving her his stamp of approval for what she was doing. He never begged, but he begged now. With her lips against his ear, her hands loving him, he knew he was in heaven.

With a gasp he sat up and opened his eyes.

Luc was alone in his bed.

Heaven had turned to hell.

He felt as if someone had taken his body and twisted it into one incredible aroused knot. He pushed himself out of bed and headed for the bathroom. Turning on the faucet, he splashed cold water on his face. He doubted even an ice bath would cool off the fire that was going on below his waist. He was as hard as a rock.

Hands planted on the counter, head hanging down, he gulped in precious air that had been missing only seconds before.

It had all been so real! Celeste had been there in bed with him, showing him what it felt like to really feel something. To allow his emotions free range as if he didn't have a care in the world other than to make love with her.

Even though the air was chilly and he was naked, he didn't feel cold.

Luc lifted his head and stared into the mirror. He didn't need to turn on a light. He'd always had excellent night vision. It helped if you were breaking into someone's house in the middle of the night.

In six hours he would be picking her up to spend the day with her. The purpose was to discuss the Prince Charming case, but he knew—he was sure they *both* knew—there was more to it than that.

How ironic that the man who vowed to not spend even five seconds with a cop was planning on spending an entire day with one.

Of course, when he made that vow he hadn't counted on a woman who provoked him into breaking too many of his self-imposed rules.

He muttered a curse and stumbled back to bed. Maybe if he fell asleep right away his haunting dream would return. For a brief second he teased himself with the question, What would have happened if his life had turned out differently? If his mother had kept him and raised him in a house filled with love and warmth. All he wanted was the chance to better his odds. Except, Luc was a realist all the way down to his bones. If he had been a privileged child, he might not have met up with Paulie and Jimmy and he wouldn't have the good life he had now.

The way he looked at it, no matter what happened there was no chance on earth for him to ever have something serious with Celeste. So he'd take what time he could get and file everything away in his memory.

Because he knew she would walk away from him. If his mother, who should have loved him, didn't want him, why would a woman it would be so easy to love, but who feared to give in to that emotion, want him?

There were too many thoughts whirling around in Luc's head for him to easily return to sleep. He lay awake and watched the faint streaks of light eventually make a path across the ceiling. He shouldn't have allowed his unconscious to conjure up the dream of what could have been. It only cemented the fact that what could have been would never be.

Considering he hadn't had a full night's sleep, Luc felt pretty alert when he parked in front of Celeste's apartment building. He guessed the building was a good thirty years old and not as well maintained as it could be. He also figured that security wasn't a major consideration here.

Celeste's apartment was on the second floor. He didn't miss the fairly new dead bolt on her door. He should have known she would choose a good one. He doubted he would have been able to pick it during his heyday as a sneak thief, and he'd had the magic touch to finesse even the most difficult lock.

He knocked and waited.

"Right on time." Celeste greeted him as she opened the door. "Coffeepot's still on if you need caffeine. I can promise you that I make a mean cup of coffee even if it doesn't resemble mud like Tank's.'' She walked through the tiny living room and into an even tinier space that doubled as a kitchen, with a bar instead of a table. She poured coffee into a large mug and handed it to him.

"Tank's coffee takes a lot of getting used to,'' Luc admitted, examining the mug. He glanced at her.

"A generic place,'' she murmured, as if there was a chance of their being overheard, "but I managed to bring along a few of my personal things. Extra-large coffee mugs are a necessity for me.''

"And these guys?'' As he sipped coffee that he agreed was excellent, he walked over to the bar and examined the two bowls sitting there. One fish, a brilliant red, swam up to the top as if to study him, too. The other fish, a deep purple with a black head, zoomed up also. "Any reason why they have separate rooms?''

"Rocky and Bullwinkle,'' Celeste said. "They're Bettas. They're also called Siamese fighting fish, which is why they have their own bowls. You put them in the same bowl, they'll fight to the death.'' She picked up a container of food and tapped a couple of pieces in each bowl. "With my schedule, it's not a good idea to have a dog or even a cat. These guys don't get cranky if I'm late getting home or have to work extra hours.''

"And they don't shed on the furniture,'' Luc murmured.

"Do you have any pets?''

He shook his head. "Like you, I don't spend that much time home. I'd probably end up killing even fish.''

"These guys are pretty hardy.''

Luc finished his coffee and watched her walk into a

small room that was obviously her bedroom. She came out holding a denim jacket that she slipped on over the rose-colored turtleneck sweater and calf-length denim skirt that topped brown boots. Her hair was more casual than the way she wore it during her hours at the bar. Now it looked tousled, as if she had merely scrunched it with her fingers when she got up that morning.

He knew she came from money, and even in these dark surroundings, she showed that wealthy background without flaunting it.

Luc had seen more than his share of the spoiled rich misses come into Dante's Cafe. And more than one of them wanted to get to know Luc Dante every which way possible. Some he'd taken to bed and promptly forgotten. He'd prided himself on not allowing anyone to have his heart.

But Celeste Bradshaw was touching something inside him.

He hungered to know more about the woman. He wanted to learn her secrets. To discover her innermost thoughts—even though he knew nothing could ever happen between them.

So why had he committed himself to the two of them spending the day together?

Because he wanted to be with her any way he could. That way, he might be able to get her out of his system without any damage to his soul. Except that he knew he had lost his heart years ago.

Once they were in his car, Celeste pulled out a notebook.

"Not yet," Luc said, switching on the engine.

"You haven't said what this day entails."

"Call it a surprise. And to protect both of us, we'll

be going out of town.'' Luc steered the car toward the highway.

''Then we can pretend to be two people out for the day,'' Celeste said, half turning in the seat. ''So tell me about yourself, Luc Dante.''

''I haven't had even a parking ticket.''

''Amazing that piece of information wasn't in any of the articles about you and your partners,'' Celeste said dryly. ''You're the poster boys for bad boys make good. You give second chances to those who are willing to work hard for one, and you don't take crap from anyone.''

''That's me.''

She narrowed her eyes as she studied him. ''Come on, Dante, throw me a bone. Tell me something about yourself.''

''The cop in you is coming out, Bradshaw.'' He deftly wove in and out of traffic.

''If I'm not allowed to ask questions, why are we doing this?''

''Because I'm kidnapping you.''

''My partner knows I'm with you and he's relentless. He'll track you down like the best bloodhound in the state.''

''The man who bets on when a supposed werewolf comes into the station? I'm shaking in my boots.'' A tiny smile touched his lips.

''Dylan's a tough guy. He has to be.''

Luc shook his head. ''I couldn't do what he does. I don't know how you can.''

''We do it because someone has to.''

''But why you? It's not as if you have to work. What prompted you to work sex crimes?''

''As opposed to what?''

"As opposed to marrying Mr. Right and raising a perfect family. You're not cop material."

Celeste looked out the window at the lush green fields courtesy of all the rain they'd had.

"I was a psychology major in college," she said. "I'd planned to go on and get my doctorate and work with children."

"But something changed your mind."

"Ellen Jameson," she replied. "She was my roommate from our freshman year on. We pledged the same sorority. We had it all planned. We'd work until we were twenty-five, then we'd marry and raise our families."

Luc sensed the shift in her mood. "Except?"

"Except in our junior year, Ellen was raped by a guy she was dating." Celeste continued looking out the car window. "It's not a new story. They'd dated a few times. She thought he was a nice guy. Except that he decided it was time to take their relationship a step further and she didn't want to. She said no, he ignored her, and she came home with torn clothing and without her virginity."

Luc breathed a silent sigh of relief. He'd expected a similar story, but with Celeste at its center.

"Police aren't always tolerant of college girls who've been raped by their dates," Celeste went on. "Or understanding or even polite. She was asked if she'd done something to provoke the guy. Had she led him on, then changed her mind? Ellen retreated while I fought on her behalf. I was so angry with them all, and I let them know it. Two months later, Ellen took a bottle of sleeping pills."

He reached for her hand and found it ice cold.

"So you became a cop to protect the Ellens in this world."

"Exactly," she said. "I got my degree and immediately entered the police academy. During my first few years, views toward date rape changed. Since Sierra Vista had recently incorporated and was hiring officers, I had an easy time getting hired on. And not because of my father," she added. "He would have done everything possible to keep me off the force. I worked hard to make detective and then I worked even harder to set up a domestic crimes unit."

"I didn't think Sierra Vista was large enough to warrant an entire unit devoted to domestic crimes," Luc said.

"Domestic crimes covers rape, domestic violence and child abuse. There are four of us. We work long hours, we're on call twenty-four hours a day, and I think we've all made a difference."

"And by doing that, you've been able to rescue Ellen again and again."

Celeste looked at him surprised. "The man knows his psychology."

"You couldn't save your friend, so you save who you can."

"Yes, I guess I do. Sierra Vista has been growing for the past few years. More families with children are moving in. We're not a sleepy little town anymore, where the worst crime was some teenage boy painting his girlfriend's name on the overpass."

"I doubt that has ever been the worst crime in Sierra Vista."

"True," she said.

"No thinking about the case," he ordered. "Let's, at least, have this morning."

"It's been so long since I've been out for the day," Celeste said.

"What do you usually do when you go out for the day?" Luc asked, curious about her.

"Oh, I pick up a variety of frozen meals that can be microwaved in the shortest amount of time, pick up my dry cleaning, cruise the drugstore, maybe pick up a video or two. If I'm feeling wild, I'll spend a couple hours at the shooting range," she said.

"No shopping at the mall, no having lunch with girl-friends, driving into San Francisco for dinner and a play?"

Celeste laughed. "I consider shopping on the same plane as going to the dentist. My friends still think I'm insane to be a cop, and the last time I was in San Francisco was to deliver a prisoner. Luc, my parents may have money, but I don't. I had to make my bed and keep my room clean. I also learned my way around the kitchen because my mother believed women should be self-sufficient. And because to this day, she can't boil water without almost melting the teapot."

"Yet you buy frozen meals," Luc pointed out.

"With my crazy hours, it's just easier. Did I tell you how much I'm enjoying working undercover at your restaurant?" she asked facetiously.

"Because of the food?"

"Definitely because of the food." Celeste looked out the window. "Where are we going?"

"I told you it's a surprise. A chance to get away."

She tipped her head to one side, watching him. "You're a very private man."

"In some places you don't feel you have anything to call your own, except your thoughts. You learn to keep to yourself. I guess that isn't something you had to worry about.''

"No, I guess not," Celeste admitted. "Although, back then, I told myself I had a horrible life. I hated myself because I had to wear braces and because I was convinced my head was too big for my body. Anytime a boy talked to me I practically broke out in hives. I admit things like that aren't earthshaking, even if they were to me at the time."

Luc shook his head in amazement. "You thought your head was too big for your body?''

"You had to be there. My dad used to say the day I turned thirteen was the day his hair started turning gray. He then said he was pushed over the edge the day I got my first bra. He said he knew things would never be the same again."

"You must have been a trip back then," Luc said.

"No, just a typical teenage girl. I didn't enter my cute stage until around age fifteen. And by then you were what, twenty-one? You wouldn't have looked at a kid like me twice."

"I spent my nights studying."

Celeste sat up straighter when she noticed the signs along the side of the road. Each advertised a different business in a tiny town called Seacrest Village that was fifteen miles away.

"We're going to Seacrest Village?" she asked, delighted. "I haven't been there in ages."

"Then, I guess I made a good choice even if isn't the best day to go there." He looked out at the gray clouds overhead.

"Then let's hope we don't end up in a downpour," she said. "With all the cloudy days and rain we've been getting, I have nightmares that I'll wake up one morning with webbed feet.''

"We've had enough rain to make some people think about building a really large boat.'' Luc turned off the highway and headed for the coast.

In no time they arrived at the small village that hugged the coastline. Geared for the tourists traveling north, the village boasted its share of antique shops, art galleries, restaurants and even a small museum of curiosities. The white painted Victorian-style buildings gave it an old-fashioned look.

Luc parked in one of the public parking lots on the edge of town. Once she stepped out of the car, Celeste buttoned up her jacket against the chilly air and pulled on gloves.

"We could go elsewhere,'' he suggested, noticing her movements.

She shook her head. "I love it like this. Besides, I won't melt.'' With a smile, she held out her hand. He wrapped his hand around hers.

"I'm glad you've decided I'm not the enemy,'' she said.

He looked down at her. Just over her shoulder he could see the storm-tossed sea, colors that were echoed in her eyes.

She was telling him to trust her.

He wanted to. That's why he had suggested their having lunch today. He hoped she would give him more information about the attacks, and that in the process, he might think of something he hadn't thought of before. He might not have known all the victims personally, but he had remembered each of them and wanted to do whatever he could to help find the criminal. He

still refused to believe anyone at the restaurant could be
a part of this.

Luc hadn't been to the picturesque village in some
time, and never with a woman. Previously, he'd come
for a quiet meal and to prowl antique shops to find
something new that would look good in the restaurant.
A year ago he'd found an elegant writing table, which
was kept out front in Dante's for the hostess to use
instead of the lectern seen in so many other restaurants.

When he suggested they get away for the day, Seacrest Village immediately come to mind. It was far
enough away that they shouldn't have any reminders of
Sierra Vista. He didn't want that intrusion. He hadn't
told Jimmy and Paulie where he was going, or with
whom. He'd prided himself on never dating a woman
who worked for him. He didn't want to hear Jimmy
give him a bad time for breaking his own rule, or see
Paulie look at him as if he was trying to figure out what
Luc was doing, just as Paulie had done many times
before. Not that Luc would have an answer for him,
because hell if he knew what he was doing. He just
needed this time with her when nothing from their lives
could interfere.

It sickened him to consider there was a connection
between Prince Charming and the restaurant. After reading about the attacks, and with the little he'd gleaned
so far from Celeste, he feared that was the case. If it
was, he wanted to do whatever he could to help. Plus,
having her all to himself today was a bonus.

"I'm surprised you didn't base your restaurant here,"
Celeste commented.

Luc shook his head. "Too touristy. I prefer having a
regular clientele. My dream was to open a place where
people will want to return. We started the Sunday

brunches two years ago and they've been very successful. Private parties have only recently been offered and have also done well.''

"I would say Jimmy's excellent cooking has something to do with it," she told him.

A corner of his lips rose. "It does, but we don't tell him that. He's big headed enough as it is."

Celeste stopped to look in a store window displaying woolen goods. A shawl draped over a rocking chair appeared to catch her interest.

"How did he get started cooking? No offense to Jimmy, but he doesn't exactly look like the kind of man to stand at a stove most of the day."

"That was pretty much thanks to Tank," Luc replied. "We worked for him one summer. Paulie and I bussed tables and washed dishes while Jimmy worked in the kitchen alongside Tank. Jimmy told Tank that there was no reason why he couldn't throw a few extra spices into his meatloaf and the hamburgers. Tank didn't laugh at him as we thought he would. He told Jimmy he could make up the daily specials for a week. If they did better, then he'd consider Jimmy's suggestions, and if they didn't, then Jimmy had to shut up and do his work."

"I've only seen Tank twice, but that does sound like him."

Luc nodded. "The guys coming into the diner liked the specials, and Jimmy was on his way. Since we already knew we wanted to start a restaurant of our own, Jimmy had a chance to experiment with dishes there. Later he took some cooking classes to learn how to make fancier dishes. Not once did we kid him for taking them."

"I wouldn't either. So Jimmy was always the brawn, you were the brains—and what was Paulie?"

"Wrong, Paulie was the brains. I was the kid everyone trusted because I could look them in the eye when I lied."

She looked up at him. "Amazing. You just told me something about yourself."

"Don't pat yourself on the back too hard, Bradshaw," he warned her. "If I tell you something, it's because I choose to. Not because you got it out of me."

Celeste shrugged. "Doesn't matter. Either way, I have another piece to add to the puzzle."

His smile was almost chilling. "Even puzzles can be deceiving. And don't forget what I said." He caught her eyes with his. "I've always been a very good liar."

Chapter 12

How many secrets did the man keep from the world? What was he holding inside that he didn't want anyone to know?

Celeste had an insatiable curiosity. More than once, it had helped her in her work, because she was relentless when she dug for the truth. Finding out about Luc Dante wasn't easy. A sealed juvenile record wouldn't allow her to find out about his past. Going through other channels hadn't given her much. And the man was elusive in talking about himself.

How many evenings had she wished for a man who didn't constantly talk about himself and his victories in business? How many dinners had she sat through where her date did everything but stand on his head to impress her? She'd reached the point where she would have *preferred* to have her date stand on his thick head.

No wonder they warned you to be careful what you wished for. She'd got it…and more.

She took one last look at the shawl in the window. She never thought of herself as one who wore shawls. That was more her mother's taste, but the color of this one fascinated her.

Perhaps she'd stop in on the way back to the car.

"I'm hoping to find some new artwork for the dining room," Luc said. "We try to change it every four or five months."

Celeste nodded. "Now that it's winter, maybe something with light. The paintings in there now are beautiful, but stormy skies are a little too close to what's outside. Sunrises or sunsets would make nice backdrops, or paintings of a clear, moonlit sky. Something that blends in as well as what you have in there now."

"True," he agreed. "I've been lucky finding what I've wanted in the galleries here." He glanced at his watch. "Lunch first?"

Celeste nodded.

"Any preference?"

"You've been here more than I have. You choose."

Luc's choice was a restored lighthouse-turned-restaurant called The Crow's Nest. One of the changes made to the building was large windows that covered the seaward side, giving the diners a view of the ocean below. Luc and Celeste were given a table by one of the windows. As Celeste was seated, Luc hung back and spoke to the hostess, who appeared to know him very well. She smiled and nodded as he slipped her something.

Celeste tamped down the jealousy that flared up inside her. When Luc joined her at the table, she smiled as if she wasn't wondering just how well the hostess knew him.

Her mother would be so proud of her.

Luc shot her a considering look.

"The clam chowder here is wonderful," he told her when the waitress stopped at their table. "It's served in a hollowed-out round of warm sourdough bread."

"Sounds perfect." She beamed.

It was just as Luc promised. Celeste found the creamy chowder thick and rich and filled with chunks of clams. She made a greedy sound after her first spoonful. She noticed that Luc was as engrossed in his meal as she was.

"This is perfect rainy day food," she told him.

"You have a menu for rainy days?"

She nodded. "Any kind of stew, chowder, mashed potatoes, hot fudge cake," she explained.

"I hope not all at once," he said.

"The hot fudge cake can pretty much be a staple. The trouble is, it's way too easy to make and I've been known to eat it all at one sitting. At least I make it in a small square pan or I'd be riding a sugar high." She dug her spoon into the chowder. "Just ask Jimmy. I never turn down dessert. What about you? Do you have a sweet tooth?"

His eyes gleamed devilishly. "I have a hankering for sweet things, yes."

Celeste felt the heat crawl up her throat and warm her cheeks. "You are a very bad man," she said.

"That doesn't bother you, does it?"

"Not where you're concerned."

Luc seemed to keep one eye on Celeste as he finished his chowder. "I gather your sweet tooth won't allow you to turn down dessert," he said when their dishes were taken away.

"Not a chance. I noticed that crème brûlée on the dessert cart and I want to see if it's as good as it looks."

Luc ordered the same, along with coffee for both of them.

Celeste hated to mar the peaceful moment, but she wanted to get work out of the way. She pulled her notebook and pen out of her bag after the waitress left their dessert and coffee.

Luc eyed the notebook warily. He set his spoon down.

"You're not wasting any time in doing your duty, are you."

"You suggested we get away today and you'd let me pick your brain. So that's exactly what I'm going to do. See if there's anything you might inadvertently know that would help our case," she pointed out. "Don't worry, this won't be long and drawn out. I thought we could do this now. I'm really hoping you might even be able to fill in some blanks."

"Blanks?"

She nodded. "We're going back to square one and questioning all the victims again in hopes something new might occur to them since our original interviews. It's still very difficult for them to talk about, so I'm hoping you can help us. If I give you a name, will you tell me what you know about the person?"

Luc nodded. "Go ahead."

Celeste glanced down at her notebook. "Barbara Miller."

"Barbara," he murmured in thought. "Very elegant, a lovely lady. She comes in about every other week or so. Usually for dinner."

"Does she come in alone or is she usually with someone?"

Luc searched his memory. "Both," he said finally.

"She's been there with a date?"

He shook his head. "I remember a few times she would bring a buyer in for drinks. She joked that one man would fly down from Seattle every time she had a show. I think it was more personal than that."

She jumped on that. "Why?"

"Body language. Dinner wasn't as leisurely with him as with other buyers," he said.

"Did you ever hear her refer to him by name?" Celeste asked as she made notes. "Or would the reservations have been made in his name so you'd have a record of it?"

Luc shook his head. "I honestly don't remember. I'm sure the reservations were always in her name, but I can check the reservations book."

"Did they come in often?"

"I'd say they came in every few months or so. But I haven't seen him in some time."

"Really?" She leaned forward. "Did you ever hear why?"

"We don't encourage gossip among the employees. But rumor had it that she learned the man was married and she ended the relationship."

"Anything else?" Celeste kept writing.

He thought for a moment. "Not really."

"Okay. What about Lauren Davis?"

"She has that candle shop in the Sequoia Art Center, doesn't she?" He waited for her confirming reply. "She used to have lunch with us about once a week."

"Used to? What changed?"

"Her divorce, which I'm sure you already know about," he said. "The last time they were in, her ex-husband created a scene. I think she's embarrassed to come back."

"She never mentioned having an argument with her ex." Celeste leafed through her notebook.

"It was more his having one with her. Lauren is very quiet, seems like a private person. Barry came in and accused her of having an affair. You only had to see the shock on her face to know it wasn't true. I escorted him out," he said with relish.

"By any chance do you remember if it happened before or after her attack?" She named the date.

"Before," he said promptly.

"You're sure?" She rolled her eyes at his expression. "Fine, you have a computer for a memory."

She suddenly felt as if that missing puzzle piece was within reach.

"Nancy Gerard and her boyfriend had a fight in the restaurant," she said. "Do you remember anything about Marie Richardson? I know she was in a relationship that ended not long ago, but she's positive her ex had nothing to do with the attack."

"She and a friend used to talk about the men in their lives at great length. I know she wasn't happy with him."

Celeste shook her head in amazement. "Is there anyone you don't know about?"

"When people eat at a place on a fairly regular basis they soon talk more freely than they might other places," he explained. "Our staff is trained to blend into the background, to serve them, to make sure they have everything they need and sometimes anticipate what they need."

"Living furniture."

"Pretty much."

Celeste studied the list of names. "They were all in a relationship of some kind," she mused. "They all ate at the restaurant on a fairly regular basis.'' Her head snapped up. Her eyes lit up with gray-green sparks. ''And they all had some kind of disagreement with their boyfriend or husband *in* the restaurant.''

All expression was wiped from Luc's face. Even his eyes turned a flat blue-black. ''Which means the restaurant *is* pivotal in your case.''

Her elation died as quickly as it had risen. While she saw the information as a positive point, another much needed lead, Luc saw it as a negative. That the business he'd worked so hard to build up could be pulled down like a house of cards.

''I could be wrong,'' she said. ''For all we know, the connection could be something else. A video store, dry cleaners, dentist.''

He shook his head. ''We both know that's not true, Celeste. It would make sense. I've read the newspaper articles on the attacks. This man thinks he's making love to the women. Maybe he thinks he's making them feel better because the men in their lives have left them.''

''And why he leaves a rose on their pillows,'' she inserted. ''In his own twisted way, he's comforting them. He wants to give them what he feels they've lost.''

''He wants to give them love.'' His statement hung between them.

Celeste slowly nodded. She looked at the window, now striped silver with falling raindrops. Beyond, the ocean waves frothed upward as they surged toward the shore. The sheer power took her breath away. She turned back to her lunch companion, who had the same power over her.

She forced herself to keep her mind on the subject at hand. It wasn't easy when she looked at him.

If it turned out his hunch was correct, then it wouldn't just be a suspicion that the restaurant was a connection. It would be a certainty.

"It's not as if these men suddenly banded together and decided to punish these women," Luc said, even his voice keeping a distance from her.

Celeste closed her notebook and tucked it back into her purse.

"I suppose you want to call your partner and give him a new heads-up," Luc said.

"I'd say Dylan would welcome any interruption since he's in court today. He hates to wear a tie," she explained. She looked out the window again. "It's days like today when I remember there's a world outside of the one I inhabit. That not everyone is a monster." She suddenly shook her head. "I'm sorry. Maudlin is not usually one of my traits."

Luc looked down at his coffee cup. "All of us have a dark side. Some more than others."

"But you actively pursue yours," she said. "You want people to see that dark and dangerous aura you project, because you think it will keep them away."

"I told you before, Celeste. I'm not a nice man."

She looked at him and wondered how many women had fallen for those bottomless dark eyes, for the fallen angel persona he projected with his dark clothing and aloof manner.

She pushed her bowl to one side and rested her arms on the table.

"What are you afraid of, Luc? Why do you keep people at arm's length as if you're afraid they'll find out about the real you?"

Luc reached into his pocket and pulled out some bills, dropped them onto the table. He pushed back his chair.

"Silence is not always a virtue," she said, following his lead.

As they left the restaurant, the hostess handed him a wrapped package. He smiled and thanked her, even as he steered Celeste out of the restaurant.

"Are you still willing to help me find artwork?" he asked.

"Of course." She mentally consigned her questions to the locked box that held so many others he hadn't answered.

It wasn't until the third gallery that they found paintings they both agreed upon. Luc purchased them and arranged to have them framed and shipped to the restaurant.

"What is the Museum of Curiosities?" Celeste asked, noticing a large two-story Victorian-style house dominating a street corner.

"The house is owned by a ninety-six-year-old woman who has an impressive collection of teapots and cups from all over the world," Luc replied. "Her husband was the captain of a freighter and always brought one back from his travels. The museum is her way of sharing them with others. Some of the pieces are one-of-a-kind. During the summer she serves tea in the gazebo behind the house. Because of her health the house is only open during the summer. I understand she's leaving it to the city with the understanding it will be kept a museum after she's gone."

Luc looked up at the sky. "We should get going before it gets dark, in case there's more rain."

"True," Celeste said, looking around. She made a mental note to return another time.

As they walked back to the parking lot, Celeste paused in front of the shop where she'd seen the shawl. She sighed when she noticed it gone from the window.

"Something wrong?" Luc asked, looking down at her.

"No." She shook her head.

The clap of thunder gave no warning. Celeste squeaked and jumped at the loud booming sound. The downpour that followed was another surprise.

"Ready to run for the car?" Luc shouted in her ear.

She nodded and took his hand. Luc disarmed the remote locks a second before they reached the vehicle.

"We're getting the seats all wet," Celeste said with dismay as she settled into the passenger seat.

"Don't worry, they'll survive," he said, grinning as he peered out the windshield. "This looks more like a squall, so it shouldn't last long." He switched on the engine, then the heater and defroster.

It took a few minutes for the heater to blast out warm air. Celeste had just unbuttoned her coat and settled back in her seat, when another clap of thunder made her jump.

"I've always hated thunderstorms," she confessed, hugging herself tightly.

Luc smiled. "So there is something that scares you."

She leaned closer to him. "The only place I thought was safe during a thunderstorm was my bedroom closet. I'd take in my favorite blanket, a flashlight and a book, and stay in there until it was over. But when I was little, my mother would come in and tell me stories. She hated thunder just as much as I did, but I never knew it back then. What did your mother do during storms?" she asked.

The distance between them could have been a million miles.

"You don't remember your mother, do you," Celeste said. "That's why you try to push me away when I ask about her."

He laughed harshly. "It's not easy to remember someone when they abandoned you after they gave birth to you."

"Oh, Luc." His name turned into a sigh.

He shook his head. "Rumor has it she was a teen living on the streets. I was always told I was better off without her."

"But you don't think so," she guessed.

"It's not a question that I'll ever have an answer to," Luc said.

Celeste leaned over and cupped his cheek with her palm.

"Do you hate her?" she asked.

"You can't hate someone you've never known," he pointed out. "Please, Celeste, I really would rather not talk about it." He moved his face so that his mouth rested against the curve of her hand. He stared at her as if to see what she would do.

She saw his unspoken challenge and accepted it. She leaned over that extra inch and replaced her hand with her lips.

As before, she sensed the coiled tension within him. She wondered what would happen if it were ever replaced. When she started to draw back, he placed his hand against the back of her head and kept her face where it was.

"Don't try to make too much of this, Celeste," he said as his mouth moved against hers. "You'd only get hurt in the end."

"No matter what you say, I don't think you'd ever hurt me." She kissed him again, the touch light and fleeting.

When Luc deepened the kiss, she melted against him. She arched against him as his hand rested lightly against her breast.

"Luc," she whispered.

"What?" His mouth was a heated brand against the curve of her neck.

She felt her lips curve upward. "Nothing."

Anything else she might have said was halted by the swift descent of his mouth on hers. Celeste felt as if she was drowning in the man. She didn't need oxygen, because he provided it. She didn't need sustenance. Only him. She tried to murmur his name again as she twisted to get even closer to him.

The clap of thunder overhead literally shook the car. The booming sound seemed to echo in their ears even afterward.

They parted and looked at each other. Both were breathing hard.

"I'm not taking that as some sign we should stop," she told him.

"We're not exactly somewhere private," Luc reminded her. He looked out the rain-streaked window. "It looks like it's let up some. We should be all right on the road." He put the car in gear.

Celeste was amazed how quickly he brought himself under control, while she was still quivering. She wondered what it would take to get him to fully drop his defenses and leave them dropped. She was ready to think of that as another challenge.

"Would you mind if I put on some music?" Luc asked as he turned out of the parking lot.

She smiled at him. ''Not at all.''

He turned on the CD player. Soft, soulful jazz poured out of the speakers. Celeste felt something deep inside her stir. She'd never considered music sexual, but there was something about this that affected her. She laid her head back against the seat and closed her eyes as she opened her mind and allowed the music to wash over her.

Sensual images danced before her. Luc's hands were hot against her face. His mouth was a searing heat against her lips while his body moved seductively against hers. What they'd just experienced was only a portent of what was to come.

Her eyes popped open and she tried to catch her breath.

There was no mistaking the heaviness in her breasts or the heat that settled deep within her belly. The images in her mind had been so sharp that her body had automatically responded.

As surely as the sun rose in the east, she knew the time would come when Luc Dante would make love to her. And when that time came, she knew she would welcome him.

She also knew that once they made love she would never be the same again.

Luc drove along the highway only half listening to the music. What caught his attention were the soft sounds of Celeste's breathing as she dozed.

Her revelation earlier that day gave him insight into why she was so passionate about her work. He'd wondered why someone with her privileged background wanted to devote her lift to such a dark area of police work. He was sure some would say that working homicide was just as dark, but he knew there were monsters out there that preferred inflicting pain to inflicting death. He knew only too well what happened in a household where money might be tight and tempers hot. He'd endured more than his share of beatings as a child, until he'd grown and been able to leave his tormentors.

He'd labeled the lady stubborn. Now he knew there was more to it. She had a core of pure steel, and he admired her for it.

Luc sensed that if anyone could find Prince Charming it would be Celeste Bradshaw. He only hoped it would happen before he fell any further.

She was beautiful to his eyes, but she was dangerous to his well-being. He was already caring too much for her.

He'd also heard rumors she was digging into his background.

Once she found out exactly who, and what, he was, he knew she would look upon him in revulsion and walk away before she was likewise tainted.

He knew the feeling only too well. It had happened once before when he'd let his guard down.

After that, he had vowed he wouldn't allow it to happen again. That vow had been easier to keep before he met Celeste.

Chapter 13

Celeste didn't open her eyes until she felt the motion of the car fully stop. When she opened them, she discovered they were parked in the small side lot next to her apartment building.

"So, what were you thinking?" Luc asked.

"Maybe I was asleep."

He shook his head. "Not a chance. The brain waves were much too active."

She decided it was a good thing he couldn't read those brain waves.

She'd used the time to try to figure out what was going on with her emotions. It wasn't easy where Luc Dante was concerned. The man had her tied up in knots.

She stared out the windshield. "The rain stopped."

Luc nodded. "We left it about ten miles outside of town. Hopefully, it was leaving town and not heading for it."

Celeste unbuckled her seat belt and half turned in her

seat so she could face him. The small space lent an intimate atmosphere that she couldn't ignore. Even more so after the roller-coaster ride her imagination had taken her on.

Maybe it was time to see if he'd take the bait or run for the hills.

"I'm handy with a speed dial and know every take-out place in town. Your choice." She served the ball into his court.

Luc remained very still as he regarded her.

"No anchovies," he said finally.

"Mushroom and sausage?"

"As long as there's extra cheese."

"Even better."

Once inside her apartment, Celeste cooed to her fish, dropped some food in their bowls and moved around in the kitchen with the phone to her ear. She placed the order as she pulled a bottle of wine out of the refrigerator.

"I'm sure it's not up to Dante's Cafe standards, but Celeste Bradley wouldn't be able to afford anything much more expensive," she told him as she poured the wine into two glasses and handed one to him.

He took a sip. "It's pretty good."

"Have a seat. If you don't mind, I'm going to change." Celeste went into her bedroom and closed the door.

Luc took the time to better study her apartment. He surveyed the rental videos stacked next to the VCR, examined the small number of books in a two-shelf bookshelf, and looked over what he called "dust collectors" that were placed at the coffee table and around the tiny room.

He easily guessed which were her personal items. Not

that they were anything expensive, but because something about the large rock painted to look like a turtle that was used as a doorstop seemed like something she would own.

In his mind, Celeste Bradshaw was a contradiction. Because of her he had to change his mind about cops. See them more as human beings. He'd heard that a few of the officers he'd had run-ins with were no longer with the force. Some were discharged because of too many infractions and others retired.

He just wished he and Celeste hadn't met the way they had.

"This is so much better," she announced, returning to the living room. She was dressed in a button-down shirt and pants in a soft-looking fleece material the color of fresh strawberries. A pair of matching socks covered her feet. She plopped down on the end of the couch and pulled a soft velvety pillow onto her lap.

"I forgot something," he said abruptly, heading for the door.

"Luc?"

He ignored her calling out to him as he quickly left the building and walked back to his car. He retrieved a package from the back seat and returned to the apartment. Celeste was still seated on the couch, but now sitting up. He handed her the package.

She looked at him for a moment, then ducked her head as she used her fingernail to slit the tape securing the paper.

"Oh." The word left her lips in a breathy sigh as she parted the papers, revealing the shawl she'd seen in the shop window that morning. She looked up. "How did you know…?"

"I saw the look on your face when you looked at it," Luc explained. "It also matches your eyes."

Celeste picked up the soft woolen fabric and rubbed it against her cheek. When she gazed up at him, the fabric mirrored the color of her eyes.

"Thank you," she murmured. "It is so beautiful."

He regretted the mood being broken by a knock on the door.

Celeste jumped up and took care of the pizza. The speed with which they ate their first piece revealed their hunger, and they didn't stop until most of the pizza was gone. Celeste refilled the wineglasses and settled back in a corner of the couch.

"Why are you afraid of me?"

Luc almost choked on his wine. He set the glass down before he dropped it.

"That's the first time I've been accused of being afraid of a woman."

"Maybe it's the first time you've been afraid of one." She held his eyes. "There's something between us, Luc. I can't ignore it and I don't think you can either—but you want to, don't you. That's what tells me you're afraid of me."

"Do you want it straight up or all wrapped up in tissue paper?" he asked.

"By now you should know I'd prefer straight up."

Luc took a deep breath. "You're a cop. Growing up on the wrong side of the tracks, so to speak, I had a reputation with the cops. If a petty theft was reported, I was on the police shortlist. If a car was taken for a joyride, you can be sure I was picked up and questioned about it. If a woman's purse was snatched and the kid who did it looked even remotely like me, I was picked up. Sometimes I felt that all I had to do was walk down the street and they'd accuse me of doing something wrong. I was the kid of a teenage hooker. I was the kid no foster family wanted. I was told I'd never come to any good. I may have proved them all wrong, but that doesn't mean I've forgiven them for preferring to arrest me instead of trying to put me on the right path. I don't have anything close to the class you were born with and I'm certainly not the kind of man who gets involved in a long-term relationship. Especially with someone like you.''

If his barb hit its mark, she didn't show it.

"I see," she said. "So even though the attraction is there, you'll refuse to go any further than you have.''

He refused to look at her. "I'm sure you can see it's for the best.''

"So the shawl was a goodbye gift?''

"Yes.''

"Liar.''

Luc's eyes blazed as his head whipped around. "I have never lied,'' he said between a clenched jaw. "Not to you, anyway.''

"You are right now.'' She draped the shawl against the back of the couch before she slid over next to him. "You weren't the first man abandoned by a teenage mother, Luc. You weren't the first kid the System let down. And you won't be the last. But you can't turn your emotions on and off just because you're afraid of being hurt.'' Just as she'd done in the car, she touched his cheek.

"It's more than that.'' He seemed to prepare himself for, if nothing else, rejection. "I was one of those abandoned babies you see on the news. I was left on a morning newspaper behind a nightclub,'' he said wearily. "One of the bartenders heard me crying and found me.'' His laughter was bitter, filled with an old pain he hadn't been able to erase. "The doctor who checked me out at the hospital came up with my name. Seems he was reading Dante's *Inferno* at the time." His eyes glowed like black coals.

Celeste sensed that if he'd ever told anyone about his beginnings, they had walked away, if not run, because no one had ever cared about him. She silently damned the teenager who would dispose of a baby the way she might a tissue. A girl who couldn't even leave him with the security of her own name. No wonder he was so closed off. He'd been rejected so many times he made sure it wouldn't happen again. She wanted to show him that where she was concerned, there would be no rejection. She leaned forward and kissed him.

"I'm very stubborn, Luc," she whispered against his mouth. "No matter what you do, I won't run away."

"Words, Celeste, just words," he said just before he returned her kiss.

She felt the tension ease just a bit. When she looped her arms around his neck, she felt him release a little more. And when she crawled into his lap, she knew she had won.

Celeste never thought of herself as greedy, but with Luc she knew she wanted it all. She pushed up his sweater and sought the warmth of his bare skin. The intense heat seemed to scorch her.

"There's no going back." His eyes were dark flames.

"That's funny, that was just what I was going to say to you." Her tongue circled the curve of his ear.

With little effort, Luc stood up with Celeste in his arms. When they reached her bedroom, he kept her in his arms as he pulled the covers back. He set her down as if she was something fragile and delicate.

''I don't break,'' she murmured, pulling him down with her.

Celeste was like a cloud of mist that surrounded Luc. How could he resist a woman whose skin was like velvet and whose mouth a sensual torment? She wasn't the least bit shy in divesting him of his clothing, tossing his sweater in one direction and his jeans in another.

''Big surprise there,'' she said with a chuckle when she looked at his black briefs. ''I swear I'm going to buy you a pair of fire-engine-red ones.''

Her tiny bikini panties and bra were a silvery-pink shade that shimmered in the dark. But it was her skin that fascinated him. He couldn't keep his hands off her as he discovered the delicate slope of her breast and flare of her hips. She echoed his every touch.

He didn't say a word during his exploration, but each touch revealed his reverence for her. When he parted the slippery pink petals and touched the tiny nubbin with his forefinger, Celeste gasped his name. But when he doffed his briefs and moved over her, into her, she cried out his name.

''You make me feel whole,'' Luc whispered as he sank into her waiting softness. ''You make me believe there can be more,'' he told her, and kissed her deeply, his tongue mating with hers.

''Then let me make it a reality,'' she said just before she flew into the heavens, with him following.

He felt like crying, just as she'd cried. She had called him horrible names. Hit him, scratched him even when he told her she'd given him a beautiful gift and he would treasure it always. He had had no idea she was a virgin. He'd gone to her only because she deserved

*a love better than the one her fiancé claimed to have
for her, even as they argued.*

*He hated leaving her when she was so distraught, but
he knew he couldn't stay. At least he kept his head and
cleaned everything up before he left.*

*Maybe once she calmed down she'd realize she was
better off having him as her first lover than the idiot
she was engaged to.*

Celeste frowned. This didn't feel right. Why wasn't
she smiling? This was one of her favorite dreams. She
was floating on a soft, fluffy cloud. The sky was a brilliant blue, and she couldn't remember the last time
she'd seen that—no rain, ditto. For the first time, she
wasn't alone on her cloud.

Her companion should make her happy, but instead,
there was something unsettling deep within her. An un-
bearable tension she couldn't remember ever feeling
was now spreading out through her body.

She turned to face her companion and recoiled.

He had no face!

That didn't frighten her as much as seeing the red
rose he held out to her. Something wet splashed onto
the back of her hand. She looked down and saw red
droplets against her skin. Blood. She opened her mouth
to scream but nothing came out. Her throat closed up
from terror. But it didn't stop her from trying to call
out, even as she tried to shake the blood from her hand.
Except, it wouldn't come off, which only terrified her
more. She whimpered as she tried again, but all it did
was flow across her hand as more blood hit her skin.
Her faceless tormentor only sat there and watched her
frenzied action.

"Make it go away! Make it go away!" she pleaded, but he did nothing.

Her voice grew high-pitched as she kept begging, and the droplets now turned into a torrent, staining her skin red.

"Celeste. Celeste!"

She was shaken almost violently.

Her eyes snapped open, but for a moment she saw nothing but the blood she was now drowning in. Her breathing was swift and shallow as she fought for air.

"Celeste! You're having a nightmare. Wake up!" This time she was shaken so hard she swore her teeth rattled.

She blinked twice and found Luc holding on to her shoulders. The expression on his face was one of pure fear.

"I—I—" She struggled to form the words. "I'm so cold."

He drew her into his arms and pulled up the blanket, draping it over her shoulders as he cradled her against his chest. She shivered violently until his body heat made her warm again.

"What in the hell were you dreaming about?" he said in her ear.

Celeste clung to him tightly. She shook her head. The last thing she wanted to do was recount what was still running in horrifying detail inside her mind.

Luckily he didn't press her but continued to hold her in his arms.

It took some time for her breathing to grow even and the terror to leave her mind.

"Let's consider ourselves lucky," she said finally.

"In what way?"

"In that when I was little and had nightmares I always threw up afterward.'' She listened to the soft rumble of his laughter.

"I am grateful for that." He was quiet for a moment. "The only way it will go away is to talk about it." She still didn't speak. Her tension vibrated all through her body. "You dreamed about him, didn't you? Prince Charming?"

"Oh, yeah." She laughed without humor. "But don't ask me who he was, since he didn't have a face, and he handed me a damn red rose that spouted blood like some insane fountain." She mumbled the words against the warmth of his chest.

"No more mushroom pizza before bed for you." He stroked her back with long calming sweeps of his hand.

After a while it didn't feel as calming as he might have planned. She could feel that tingle start up again. She half sat up so she could see his face.

"You know," she said huskily, "I've heard that sometimes physical activity can chase nightmares away better than anything."

"Really?"

She nodded. "Maybe if I had something to take my mind off it..." She allowed her voice to trail off suggestively.

Before she could blink she found herself sprawled across Luc's chest as he adjusted her to sit astride his hips.

"It will be a pleasure to do anything I can to help you take your mind off your bad dream," he said.

"Such a gentleman." She was leaning down to kiss him when her phone jangled. She froze. Keeping her eyes locked on his, she reached over and grabbed the handset.

"Hello?"

"Wakey, wakey, babe. I'll pick you up in ten."

"Another one?" Celeste felt Luc freeze under her.

"Yeah. She's at the hospital now. So throw on some undies and outies and be out front." Dylan hung up.

Celeste hit the off button and put the handset down. She slid off Luc and got up.

"I heard enough," Luc said as he straightened and pushed himself out of the bed.

"Damn, they're happening closer together," she muttered, rummaging through a drawer and pulling out underwear. She wasted no time in dressing in jeans and a heavy fleece top. She'd just tied the laces to her running shoes when she looked up. "This is the way my life is. They call. I go."

Uncaring that he was still naked, he knelt in front of her and took her hands in his. He rubbed them briskly.

"Right now you need to concentrate on your case," he said in a low voice.

Her smile was resigned. "Yes, I do. Help yourself to coffee or whatever you can find. I probably won't be back for a few hours."

Luc nodded. "If you need tonight off, give me a call." He stood up and walked over to the pile of clothing, part of it his. He dressed quickly.

Celeste looked out the window and saw Dylan's car glide to the curb.

"I have to go." She retrieved her weapon from the lock box and attached her badge to her waistband. "You only need to set the dead bolt when you leave. It automatically locks behind you."

"I'll walk you out."

"No." She shook her head. "No." She started for the door, then spun around, wrapping her arms around him and kissing him with the heat he'd become so familiar with. He tasted her hunger, and something else that called out to him. An emotion he'd always turned his back on—but couldn't with her. Before he could attempt to deepen their kiss, she stepped back, then ran for the door. She was gone before he could utter a word.

Luc walked over to the window and looked down. He soon saw Celeste running out of the building and over to Dylan's car. He didn't expect her to look up before she got into the vehicle. So why did he feel disappointed when she didn't?

Celeste in his arms had been more than anything his dreams had foretold. She wove magic around him that warmed his cold soul. Then she'd sought him for comfort after her nightmare. Just the little she'd told him was chilling. He didn't want to imagine what it would be like to have that horror presented in living color.

Now that she was gone, he saw no reason to stay.

Luc made sure the dead bolt was engaged and that it locked behind him.

He had known making love with Celeste would change his life. From the first time he'd kissed her he'd felt something come alive deep down inside him. The darkness that seemed to hover around him even appeared lighter. But that uncertainty still haunted him— that even if she was the bright spot on his horizon right now, she might not be there for him tomorrow. It wasn't going to be as easy for him from now on. Before, he hadn't minded being alone. Now he didn't think he would feel as comfortable with it as he once had.

"You sounded pretty alert when I called," Dylan said, parking the car in the parking lot near the Emergency Room.

"Bad dreams," she said, as he coasted to a stop and she climbed out.

"Really?" He didn't sound convinced. She was relieved he didn't pursue it.

Early-morning hours didn't mean the ER wasn't busy. Dylan checked at the front desk, then they headed for the rear.

One of the doctors saw them and walked over.

"It's not good," he said. "She was hysterical when they brought her in, so I had to sedate her. I didn't give her enough to knock her out. Just enough to relax her."

"Anything you can tell us now?" Celeste asked.

"I can tell you that Stacy Nash fought back," he said. "As a result, she has a black eye, a split lip, and bruising along the inner thighs, her breasts and on one wrist that's also sprained. No sign of semen. She mentioned she'd scratched him, but it looks like he even cleaned under her fingernails. Samples were taken under her nails, but they looked pretty clean." He took a breath. "The sad part about this whole thing is that she was a virgin. She'd planned on waiting until her wedding night."

"Oh no," Celeste murmured.

"Her fiancé is back there with her, and he's taking it pretty bad." He grimaced. "He's ready to kill the guy who hurt her. I'd say he's a time bomb, ready to go off at any second."

Dylan muttered a pungent curse under his breath.

"He giving you too much grief?" he asked the doctor.

"Nothing we haven't had before," the doctor replied. "He wants to lash out at someone, and right now we're all he has."

They didn't need directions to the correct curtained cubicle. They only had to follow the sound of cursing.

Celeste said Stacy's name before stepping around the curtain. "Stacy?" She walked up to one side of the gurney. "I'm Detective Celeste Bradshaw. This is Detective Parker." She didn't miss the slightly glazed look in the young woman's eyes. She ignored the young man standing nearby.

"I want that son of a bitch for hurting her," he snarled. "If I find him first, he'll be in pieces by the time I finish. Look what he did to my baby! Why haven't you caught him yet?"

Stacy whimpered as she looked at her fiancé.

"Let's take a walk, shall we?" Dylan took his arm and pushed him out of the cubicle.

Stacy had the blank gaze of someone under heavy medication as she looked at Celeste. "He hurt me," she whispered.

"I am so sorry," Celeste said gently. "I know this isn't easy for you, but I'd like to ask you a few questions." She carefully guided the woman through the night's events. Even sedated, Stacy gave a concise statement as to what had happened.

"You know what was weird?" She slurred her words. "He smelled like oranges."

Celeste's head snapped up. "Smelled like oranges?" she repeated.

"Yes." Stacy licked her lips. "Jason had given me some orange bath oil, and all I could think of was that his hands smelled like my bath oil."

Celeste suspected the bath oil would be in the trash when Stacy returned home.

"Tell Jason he can't go after this man," Stacy

begged. Tears appeared in the corners of her eyes. "I know he sounds tough, but I'm afraid he'd get hurt."

Celeste took a tissue and dabbed at her eyes. "We'll talk to Jason," she said. "I will come see you later in the day."

"It hurt so much," Stacy whimpered. "He wouldn't stop. He said he was making love to me. That's not love, is it?" Her eyes drooped.

"No, Stacy, it's not." Celeste tucked her card into Stacy's hand and left.

She found Dylan and Jason standing outside the ER. Judging from the look on her partner's face, he had his hands full keeping the hotheaded young man in line. She walked through the sliding doors, hearing Jason's voice first.

"Why haven't you caught this bastard yet?" he exploded at Dylan. "Stacy's delicate! This isn't something she should have to live with for the rest of her life, and now she has to because you idiots can't do your job! Let me tell you, if you can't find him, I will, and by the time I'm finished with him you won't have to worry about a trial!"

Celeste didn't remember moving her feet. Only that one moment she was just outside the ER entrance and the next she had her hand planted against Jason's chest.

"Listen to me very carefully, Jason," she told him between gritted teeth. "The woman you love, the woman you have promised to cherish for the rest of your life, has been brutally attacked, and you're ranting and raving about catching her attacker." She pushed him hard enough that he almost lost his balance. "Do you really want to help us? Then do the right thing. Be thankful she is still alive and tell her you will do everything in your power to help her get through this. You leave the task of catching the rapist to us while you give Stacy all the time and all the love she needs to heal physically and emotionally. You do not leave her side, do you hear me? Because if you don't to as I say, so help me God, I will make your life a living hell.''

She was sure the fire shooting from her eyes left him in no doubt of her words.

''Trust me, man, she can do it,'' Dylan said calmly, seeming unaffected by her attack.

Celeste kept her eyes on Jason, who now looked panicked.

''So, tell me, Jason, what are you going to do?'' she asked in a quiet voice that was just as deadly.

''Be with her,'' he gasped. ''Help her. Please, I can't breathe!''

She backed away, her hand dropping to her side. ''Good idea.''

Jason took one last look at her and almost ran for the entrance.

''You sure put the fear into him,'' Dylan commented. ''Nothing like an angry woman to put a guy in his place.''

Celeste took several deep breaths to calm her racing pulse.

''I can't believe I did that,'' she muttered. ''No matter how angry I have gotten with someone I have never put my hands on them.''

Dylan rested his hands on her shoulders and studied her. ''You're not going to cry, are you? Damn, Leste, you know I can't handle tears. Hey,'' he crooned, ''everything's fine. He was a jerk, and now he just might not be one—all thanks to you.''

She blinked rapidly. ''Stacy Nash is a medicated mess, Dylan. She's now convinced that sex hurts. That while a guy might say all the right words, it can't be beautiful.'' *Not like last night with Luc.*

''Then let's hope the time comes when she realizes Jason isn't Mr. Wonderful and she sends him on his way,'' he said. ''Come on, Killer, let's head for the station and see what's waiting for us.'' He peered at her closely. ''You look different.''

''Too many middle-of-the-night calls,'' she told him, deftly steering him toward the car.

Celeste longingly thought of her bed, and Luc in it. Unfortunately, she knew even if she returned to the apartment at this very minute she wouldn't find him there.

She wondered how he would act toward her that evening. Would he prefer to forget everything that had happened, or would he drag her into his office and lock the door?

Judging by the simmering heat deep within her belly, she'd be the one dragging him into his office and locking the door.

Chapter 14

"Let's stop by and see Carl this morning," Dylan suggested. "See if the guy was out partying last night."

"Sounds good to me."

"So, what did you learn from Dante yesterday?" he asked.

That making love with the man will make you forget everything.

"Something besides the restaurant is the connection," she replied. "He remembered the victims, and he also remembered that each of them had a fight with their significant other while eating there."

Dylan snapped his fingers. "Which would make an excellent reason for the rapist to think he's doing them a favor, in his sick and twisted way."

She nodded. "He sees them as women in pain and he wants to make them feel better."

Dylan pulled the car over to the side of the road. "Which could actually mean that Carl might not be our guy. It would have to be someone who's around there when the restaurant's open. Carl's in there when it's closed.''

''Unless he's also eaten there,'' Celeste pointed out. ''Another thing. Stacy Nash said her attacker smelled like oranges—specifically his hands. She said she remembered it because his hands smelled like some bath oil she'd been given.''

Dylan noticed the expression on her face. ''And?''

''And the soap used in the Dante's Cafe rest rooms is orange-scented. It should have occurred to me before, but it didn't. It's not something exclusive, but it isn't something you'll find just anywhere.''

''There's still no one working there who shows up even as a Peeping Tom,'' Dylan said, looking frustrated.

''He works there, Dylan,'' she said. ''I don't think he's one of the customers. He's one of the employees. And we can smoke him out.''

''Really? How?''

''I'm going to let the men there believe I've had a fight with my boyfriend. I'll act down in the dumps and, if asked, I'll cry a few tears and lament over the no-good bum.''

''What if he needs to see a confrontation?'' Dylan asked.

''Let's try this out first,'' she said, growing more enthusiastic.

Dylan shook his head. ''I don't know.''

''It's a shot.''

He still didn't look convinced. ''It could also get dangerous if he gets wind of you being a cop.''

''I'm working tonight. I'll start on it then.''

''I still want to stop by and see Carl when the nursery opens,'' Dylan said.

"Fine with me." Celeste pulled out her notebook and charted the dates of each rape. "Have you noticed that the time between attacks is getting shorter. Going by this pattern the next one could be any night now."

Dylan nodded. "And the violence is escalating. The next death might not be an accident."

"Which is why we need to catch him before he strikes again. The soap may be a clue, but the staff have their own rest rooms off the kitchen."

"No fancy orange-scented soap for the help?"

She had to think a moment. "No."

"What about the partners? We never really took them off our list."

"Jimmy has a girlfriend."

"That's never stopped anyone."

"He doesn't really fit the profile of a sweet, caring lover who sees to their needs," she said.

Dylan quickly changed lanes. "And the other guy?"

"Paulie is the sensitive type, but he's very shy around women."

"Which would make him perfect. Why have we not checked into him further?" he demanded.

"Because neither man fits," she argued. "And why this sudden interest in Paulie? Luc would know if one of them was the rapist. Not physically know, but he'd sense it."

Dylan spared a quick glance at her. He groaned when she flushed. "You slept with him! You slept with the guy!"

"Paulie isn't my type," she said primly, even as her stomach performed a few quick somersaults.

"You know very well I meant Luc Dante. That's why you sounded so awake when I called. He was there!"

Celeste was grateful they had pulled into the station

parking lot. She knew Dylan wouldn't presume to lecture her around fellow officers.

"He's not a suspect, but that doesn't mean what you did was a good idea," he told her in a fierce whisper. "We're working an important case, Bradshaw." He only called her by her last name at the station, or if he was royally ticked off at her.

"Back off, Parker," she shot back.

Dylan shook his head. "I just hope you know what you're doing."

Celeste didn't reply that she hoped the same.

The moment they reached their desks, Celeste scanned messages while Dylan ran another check on Paulie and Jimmy. He grumbled that he had to wait until a fairly respectable hour before calling contacts. If he was up, there was no reason why they couldn't be awake, too.

"Man, Parker, you must still have the hots for your ex-wife," Davidson, one of the detectives, joked as he passed their desks.

"The last person I'd have the hots for is that she-devil," he declared.

Celeste and Dylan noticed the few milling around all had broad grins on their faces.

"What's the joke?" she asked.

Davidson dropped a newspaper on her desk. He didn't have to point to a particular article. It was already circled in red.

"Yep, a real generous guy," he chuckled, sauntering off.

"What?" Dylan demanded, seeing the expression on her face.

"How did you pay Alexa her alimony this month?" she asked.

"I wanted her to work for it. I sent her a hundred scratch-off lottery tickets."

Celeste handed the newspaper to him. Dylan's face turned purple as he read the article.

"Parker, say something—before you explode."

Dylan shoved back his chair and stood up. He stalked off without a word.

"Is it true?" One of the clerks came up to Celeste. "Did Parker's ex-wife win fifty thousand dollars from a lottery ticket he'd given her as part of her alimony?"

Celeste looked at the newspaper that now lay shredded on Dylan's desk. "It's true."

"I wish my ex would do something like that. Except with him, I'd probably be lucky to win a free ticket." She handed papers to Celeste. "Preliminary crime scene report. They know everything on this is a rush."

"Thanks, Risa." She scanned the contents. By now, she should be disheartened to learn it was pretty much the same as all the others, but she looked at it another way. At least it wasn't the work of a copycat, which meant she didn't have to worry about tracking down another rapist.

When Dylan returned, he looked calmer. He set a coffee container on her desk along with a muffin.

"No one's made fresh coffee here yet," he announced.

"Thank you." She picked up her coffee and sipped it. "Prelim crime scene report." She handed it over to him. "Nothing different."

Dylan glanced at his watch. "The nursery should open in an hour. Let's head out there then."

Celeste glanced at the papers littering her desk. "Maybe I can make some headway here before we leave.'' She then noticed the pile hidden behind the computer monitor. ''Or not.''

By the time they left the station, Celeste felt she'd gotten some work done.

''Why in the world did you give Alexa one hundred lottery tickets? Didn't you stop to think the odds might be in her favor?'' she asked on the way to the nursery.

Dylan's knuckles turned white as he gripped the steering wheel. ''I haven't even won a free ticket any time I've picked up one of those damn things.''

''Then realize you can't get the best of her and don't try any more tricks. So far they've pretty much backfired on you,'' she advised, unbuckling her seat belt when Dylan stopped the car in front of Thatcher's. ''Just write a damn check!''

''Boy, for someone who had a hot night, you're sure cranky,'' he grumbled.

''I could report you for sexual harassment.''

Dylan made an impolite noise. ''Like you haven't said worse to me.''

''You are such a juvenile,'' Celeste muttered, even as she pasted an impersonal smile on her lips.

''Bite me, Bradshaw.''

''Only after I have my rabies shot.''

By the time they entered the nursery grounds, no one would have known they'd been arguing like preschoolers.

''Well, look who's here.'' Mrs. Thatcher greeted them. ''I figured you'd want to talk to Carl, so I told him to hold off leaving just yet. You better be quick about it. We lose money when he's not out there.'' She turned her head. ''Carl! Those two cops are here to see you.''

"What made you think we'd be back out here, Mrs. Thatcher?" Dylan asked.

"Easy. You think he's Prince Charming, what with the roses and all." She sniffed. "That boy may know his way around flowers and shrubs, but he don't know a thing about women."

Celeste and Dylan exchanged a look when the object of their conversation walked from a greenhouse in the back.

If Celeste had to describe a typical ninety-pound weakling she would describe Carl Thatcher. The young man was so thin she was positive if he stood sideways he would disappear completely. Sandy-colored hair hung lankly around his ears and forehead, and washed-out-blue eyes regarded them warily.

She bet he was the perfect target for bullies in school.

"Mr. Thatcher." She did the greeting, sensing he would respond better to her than to Dylan. "I'm sure your mother told you we've been checking on some of the businesses you service."

He twisted his hands nervously. "I just do my job and leave. I don't take nothin'."

"Have you ever noticed anything odd going on? We understand you supply roses to restaurants such as Dante's Cafe. Has anyone ever requested a larger number than usual?"

He shifted from side to side. "Sometimes. A guy wants to look good and give his girlfriend a rose, so he asks me to just tack a few on to an order."

"Anyone in particular?"

Now he looked just plain scared. "I did nothin' wrong."

"No one said you have," she soothed. "We're not accusing you of anything, Mr. Thatcher."

"Just tell her anything you know, Carl." Mrs. Thatcher used her voice like a whip. "You've got deliveries to make."

"Dante's Cafe gets extras sometimes. In case something happens to one of them at a table or to give out for a woman's birthday or somethin'. That day spa gets extras sometimes like Valentine's Day or Mother's Day."

"Do you just deal with one person at each business?" Dylan asked.

Carl refused to look at him, but they knew the man wasn't lying. He didn't have the courage to lie, especially in front of his mother. He nodded.

"Who?" Celeste asked.

"Wanda Mason at the spa, Paulie at Dante's Cafe, Richard Sinclair at that women's lingerie store. They give out roses on sale days," he went on to explain.

"Thank you, Mr. Thatcher." She smiled warmly and offered her hand. He hesitated, then quickly wiped his hand on his pants before taking hers. "We're sorry if we kept you from your duties. We just wanted to clear up a few things."

He nodded jerkily, then practically ran back to the greenhouse.

Mrs. Thatcher sighed deeply. "Takes after his father. That man was about as spineless as a jellyfish," she declared.

"Thank you also," Celeste said.

"I told you he wasn't no Prince Charming," the older woman said.

"That's an understatement," Dylan said to Celeste as they returned to their vehicle. "Just do me a favor? Tonight, will you keep an eye on Paulie? See if he acts different than he does any other night."

"See if he has any visible scratches," she added. "Too bad he thought to clean under her nails. We would have had prime DNA that way. I'll see what I can pick up."

She didn't want to think Paulie was Prince Charming, but as she thought about it, she could see why Dylan suddenly considered him a prime suspect. Paulie did fit the profile. She hadn't looked closely at him because nothing in his file indicated he would do such a thing. But then, who could say he hadn't changed over the years? And he'd always talked about his status as the quiet member of the trio....

Maybe this quiet one wanted to be noticed, too.

"So what did you do on your day off?" Jimmy asked when Luc walked into the kitchen. He headed for the coffeepot and poured himself a cup. "You know, we're not used to you actually taking time for yourself."

"I drove out to Seacrest Village," Luc replied. "Looked for new artwork for the dining room. Had lunch." *Made love with the most incredible woman in the world.*

"At least you didn't make it all business." Jimmy checked a sauce simmering in a pot.

"How was it here?" Luc leaned against a counter and watched his friend work.

"Quiet."

Luc felt heat spreading across the back of his neck just as Celeste stepped through the rear door. He straightened up when he noticed she wore the shawl he'd given her draped around her shoulders. The smile she offered him showed no sign that she'd come apart in his arms more than once last night.

"Hey, Blondie," Jimmy greeted her. "We got a shipment of wine in today you'll need to double-check. I left the invoice on the bar for you.''

''I'll take care of it immediately.'' She disappeared into the break room and came out looking ready for work.

Luc waited a few minutes before following her. Celeste stood at the bar studying the invoice. She glanced up when he entered.

''Thank you for making sure the dead bolt was secured,'' she said.

''You asked me to.'' He set his coffee cup on the bar. ''Jimmy had them put the wine down below.''

She nodded. She chewed on her lower lip. ''Have Jimmy or Paulie said anything about what they did yesterday?''

''Since the restaurant was open and I wasn't here, I would assume they worked.'' He stopped and stared at her. ''Wait a minute. There is no way in hell you can think either one of them had something to do with that attack,'' he whispered fiercely.

''More things have come up,'' she murmured. ''Think about it, Luc. I'll be honest with you. With what we have, if you didn't have a rock-hard alibi for last night, you would have come under suspicion, too.''

''Of course. It's easier to think of me that way, isn't it.''

''That's not it and you know it,'' Celeste argued, keeping her voice low. She wanted to tell him she was falling in love with him, but she sensed in his frame of mind he wouldn't believe her. After all, no one had loved him before, so why would it happen now?

''The princess and the mongrel.''

''I don't give a damn about your parents. I don't give

a damn about your past. Just your present, and I'd like to see a future.'' Her eyes blazed silvery-green lights.

He kept shaking his head. ''Forget it, Celeste. Yes, last night was great, but when this is all over, you'll be thankful I didn't ask for more. As for Jimmy or Paulie, you're way off base.'' He held up his hand. ''I don't want to hear any more. You and I are done.'' He didn't look back as he left the restaurant.

Celeste blew out an exasperated breath. ''Stubborn idiot,'' she muttered, unconsciously crumpling the invoice in her hand. She winced when she realized what she'd done, and carefully smoothed out the paper.

Since she'd come in early, she decided she wanted a little time to herself. She decided to be brazen, and headed for Luc's office. Once there, she closed the door and settled herself behind his desk. Comfortably ensconced in the soft leather chair, she imagined the warmth of his body curved around her. She even caught a hint of his scent in the air.

Celeste was still hurt that Luc thought they were over. She knew it was going to be a long, hard road to convince him otherwise. Why did she have to fall in love with such a hardheaded man? He'd already proven to be more complicated than a Chinese puzzle.

''You never liked things easy, did you?'' she said. Whether she was speaking about herself or about Luc was another question.

She hadn't meant to, but she found herself idly sifting through the paperwork neatly arranged on his desk.

''What the hell do you think you're doing?''

Celeste looked up to find Jimmy looming over her. He snatched the papers off the desk.

''I knew something was going on between you two,''

his voice boomed. "I could see it the minute you came in tonight. But let me tell you, honey, it won't lead to anything. If you think you got him hooked, think again. Luc's too smart to be used. He might sleep with you for the thrill of it, but it won't be anything more than that."

Her stomach churned at his words because she suspected they could be true. Even in the face of Jimmy's fury, she felt no fear. She couldn't imagine his being Prince Charming. A man with his temper would have left Stacy Nash in even worse condition. She wasn't going to take any chances, however, so she kept an eye on the paperweight near her hand. Just in case she needed to defend herself.

"You don't know what's going on," she said calmly.

"Yeah, I know—a cute girl thinks she'll get a free ride. It's not going to happen, honey, because you're fired," he told her.

"What is all this yelling about?" Paulie appeared in the doorway.

Anytime Luc needed to be by himself, he drove. After leaving the restaurant, he got in his car and drove without giving a thought to his destination. He needed to be away from Celeste. He needed to think.

He had to have been nuts to admit he was falling in love with her. He wasn't meant for love. Didn't she realize that?

Yet she knew all about him and it hadn't scared her off. She knew what his past was like and that didn't repel her at all.

And, God help him, he *was* falling in love with her, because even his pragmatic self said she was about the best thing in his world.

He couldn't understand why she thought Jimmy or Paulie could be the rapist. Jimmy sure couldn't be. He wouldn't think to leave a rose on a victim's pillow. Jimmy never remembered to give his girlfriend flowers for her birthday unless he or Paulie reminded him.

It wouldn't be Paulie, either. Anytime a woman talked to him about more than the weather, Paulie practically stumbled over every word he uttered.

Luc thought back to when they were hell-raising teenagers. Luc and Jimmy were always competing for the girls. Paulie even once said...

He suddenly doubled over as if he'd been punched. Sickening clarity brought back a long-forgotten memory. Grateful he had his cell phone clipped to his belt, he quickly punched out the phone number for the restaurant. No one answered. He tried another phone number after that.

"Dylan Parker."

Luc took a quick breath to keep the sick feeling from spilling over. "It's Dante. There's something I need to tell you."

Chapter 15

"What is going on here?" Paulie looked from one to the other as he stood in the doorway.

Jimmy shook his head and pointed at Celeste. "I caught her looking through Luc's paperwork. If you'd seen them earlier you'd know that something happened between them. I just bet Luc wasn't alone yesterday. You were with him, weren't you?" he demanded of Celeste.

"You don't understand," she said.

Jimmy muttered an uncomplimentary description of her. Paulie didn't back down, but verbally attacked the larger man. Celeste wisely stayed out of it but kept an eye on both of them. Even then, she was unprepared when Jimmy hit Paulie in the face and pushed him out of his way as he stalked out of the office.

"Are you all right?" she asked Paulie, leading him to a chair.

He held his hands over his nose, which was bleeding

profusely. "I don't think it's broken. I've had a broken nose before."

"Tip your head back. I'm going to get something for it," she told him. She practically ran for the rest room, wet some paper towels and brought them back. "I'd get some ice, but I don't think it's a good idea for me to go into the kitchen right now." She gently moved his hands away, winced at the bruising that was already blooming and carefully wiped the blood from his face. "Thank you for standing up for me."

He smiled, then groaned as the motion pained him. "He didn't need to call you that."

"He's angry."

Paulie looked up at her. "You don't need to stay here right now while you're feeling upset. Let me take you home." He waved off her protests. "Please."

She managed a smile. "Okay."

Paulie took her out to his car and tucked her into the passenger seat. She welcomed the blast of warm air after he started up the engine.

"Are you dating Luc?" he asked once he'd pulled into the street. "It's all right with me. You have to understand that Jimmy's protective about both Luc and me. He's like our big brother. We sort of watch over each other. For a long time we were the only family we had."

"With Luc, it's complicated," Celeste replied. "We were arguing earlier. Who knows, maybe the vibes stuck around and Jimmy picked up on them." She looked down at her lap, only to find her hands twisting one way then the other. She quickly relaxed them.

"Don't worry about what Jimmy said. You're not fired," he assured her. "If nothing else, you're way too good a bartender. He'll cool off and later on, I wouldn't be surprised if he even apologizes to you.''

''I promise not to expect an apology,'' she said.

Paulie looked at her with what she would have described as puppy-dog eyes. ''You deserve so much, Celeste. You deserve to be cherished. To be given beautiful roses and told how much you're appreciated.''

You deserve. Every victim she'd spoken to had told her that the rapist had said they deserved love or deserved to be loved. No matter what the phrase was exactly, he always used the word *deserve.* Alarm bells went off inside her head.

Dylan was right.

She licked her lips, which suddenly felt very dry.

Maybe it was coincidence. Just because Paulie used that phrase didn't mean he was the rapist. She told herself she was giving in to her suspicious nature, but it didn't stop the prickles of unease traveling down her spine.

It wasn't until he parked in front of her building that she realized she hadn't given him the address or even directions. She carefully kept her features blank.

''Thank you for the ride,'' she said, striving for a normal tone. ''You're right. It was better that someone else drove me.''

Paulie climbed out and walked around to the passenger side, opening the door.

''I can see myself in,'' Celeste assured him.

''There's no way I'd let you go in by yourself.''

She swiveled her hips and got to her feet. ''I didn't want to take you from your work any more than I needed to.'' She managed to present him with a smile. ''I'm going to go inside, change my clothes, fix myself a cup of hot tea and unwind.'' *And call Dylan and talk this over with him.*

Paulie circled his fingers around her wrist so that she couldn't move away.

''Luc wouldn't like it if I didn't make sure you got in safely.''

Having no argument to his statement, she allowed him to guide her inside the building. She almost asked him how he knew which apartment was hers, but she already knew he would have a ready answer. When she unlocked the door and started inside, she tried to block his entrance, but Paulie was too fast. He was inside before she could blink. He closed the door behind him.

''You know, don't you?'' He sounded sad and resigned. ''I shouldn't have mentioned the roses.''

She could have tried to lie her way out of it, but decided against it.

''Yes, I do,'' she said quietly. ''Paulie, I'm a police detective investigating the rapes. Let me help you.''

His shoulders slumped. ''I thought you were too good to be true.'' He suddenly straightened. Celeste realized she wasn't looking at the quiet man she'd gotten to know since that first day she'd met him at the restaurant.

''Paulie, you can't make things right, but you can do what's right,'' she insisted.

He shook his head as he pulled her toward the center of the small living room. She tried to pull back, but he showed a strength he hadn't revealed before.

''No one knows we're here,'' he told her. ''Both Luc and Jimmy left the restaurant before we did. Jimmy knew I was on my way out. I'm sorry, Celeste, but I can't let you ruin things for me. For them. The scandal would destroy what we've built up.'' He looked around.

"Prince Charming usually strikes late at night, but I guess things could change."

Celeste forced her panic down. She knew she needed to keep her wits about her because Paulie wouldn't allow this victim to survive the attack. Her first thought was to let loose a healthy scream, but she knew everyone living on this floor worked during the day, and while the building was old, it was well insulated. She never heard a sound from her neighbors the evenings she was home.

"Believe me, Paulie, you don't want to do this." She squirmed in an attempt to escape, but his grip was too strong. If she survived this, she was sure to have bruises.

He looked at her sadly. "I have no choice."

"You have plenty of choices! What you're thinking of doing will only make things worse," she pointed out. "You have to know they'll catch you. My partner is like a pit bull. He doesn't stop until the case is solved. Plus there's Luc. We may have fought, but you have to know how this would affect him, too!"

"Sure, he'll be hurt for a while, but Jimmy and I will be there for him. The time will come when he won't even remember your name."

Celeste vainly pulled on his hand.

Paulie looked toward the bedroom. Celeste noticed the direction of his gaze and pulled all the harder. He ignored her efforts.

"I never hurt any of those women," he said. "You didn't see them when they were in the cafe with men who didn't appreciate them. I wanted the women to feel loved."

Her temper flared up even more at his words.

"You didn't love them! You raped them!" she

yelled. "You broke in to their apartments or houses and, by God, you raped them! You took away their sense of self! One woman was so traumatized she had a heart attack and died. Another was a virgin, but she fought back, didn't she? She didn't want you to touch her!" She clawed at his arm. The sleeve slipped up and she saw scratches on his arm. "That's what Stacy Nash did to you." She intended to inflict her own hurt, and raked her nails down his arm. Tiny specks of blood appeared on his skin. A fierce part of her gloried in the knowledge she'd left marks, while her training reminded her if he wasn't as careful as before, at least she would have evidence for Dylan to work with.

A terrifying light appeared in his eyes as he practically pushed his face against hers. "You are *wrong*. I gave them the romance they didn't get from those idiots in their lives. I understand what a woman wants, but do they bother with me? No! Women don't even look at me once. They'll look at Luc, or even at Jimmy, but they always ignore me. Luc didn't want a woman to love because he thought they wouldn't love him. Jimmy thinks Valentine's Day is for wimps. But I knew what I wanted for women. I wanted to give them what they never had before. I wanted to give them a lover who could cherish them."

Celeste's thoughts raced through her mind. If something didn't happen soon, there was an excellent chance she was going to be Prince Charming's next victim. Dylan would have to work the case alone. What would happen with Luc? How would he handle the news of her death? Would he realize what he'd lost? She felt her throat tighten up at the thought of the man she loved.

"No one will believe it's an accident." She spoke

swiftly, struggling to keep desperation out of her voice. The last thing she wanted to show Paulie was any sign of weakness. "You know Luc and Jimmy will ask questions. They'll probably even suspect you had something to do with it. Jimmy knows you were at the restaurant when he left. He might even wonder how I got home. What will you do when they start asking you questions you can't answer? Will you kill them, too?" She hammered the words at him. "Tell me something, Paulie— will you kill your two best friends? The men you consider your family? They won't cover up for you. You know they won't."

"It won't come to that," he argued.

"How do you know?" She ruthlessly continued. She pulled on his hand in hopes she could get loose, but he kept his grip tight. "You've killed once. Each time you kill, it just gets easier to do it another time."

"Shut up, Celeste." He walked into the bedroom and pushed her so hard she lost her balance and fell on the bed.

Freed of constraints, Celeste had pushed herself upward, ready to claw, scream and kick, when she heard a roar and watched Paulie fly through the air. The man landed hard on the floor, with a furious Luc looming over him.

"You son of a bitch!" Luc snarled, reaching for him again. He drew his fist back, ready to inflict more pain.

"Luc, no!" Celeste cried out. She already saw the fear in Paulie's eyes and knew the man would meekly accept whatever punishment Luc meted out. "Please, Luc, don't." She crawled across the floor and grabbed his arm. She could feel the muscles quivering under her hands. "Look at him," she implored. "He isn't going to fight back."

Luc slowly lowered his arm to his side. He reached down and pulled Celeste up into his arms. He held her so tight she mumbled a protest.

"Luc, I need to breathe," she murmured against the warmth of his neck as she clung to him.

They both looked down at Paulie, who had pushed himself up against the wall. With his hands covering his face, Paulie sat there crying like a small boy.

"He's broken, Luc," she said softly. She raised her head at the sound of police sirens from outside. She smiled as she heard Dylan shouting at a patrol officer.

Luc kept her in his arms. "I remembered something," he said simply.

"How long are you going to sit around looking like that?" Dylan asked Celeste a week later.

"Looking like what?"

"Like you lost the guy you're in love with."

Pain sliced through her. "I arrested his best friend for rape. Luc hasn't even called me, so how can you honestly think he'll want to see me?"

"Sure he will," he said confidently. "You forget. He called me to tell me he realized that there was a good chance Paulie was Prince Charming. For some reason he remembered ordering those particular roses was Paulie's idea. The guy said something about how a woman deserved a beautiful rose. He drove back to the restaurant and found Paulie's car gone and yours still there. He called me and said he was on the way to your apartment. He had a hunch that's where the two of you were headed. The guy sounded scared, and something tells me he never gets scared. Go see him, Celeste. If he's stupid enough to toss you out on your butt, I promise I'll go back and beat the crap out of him. Fair enough?"

She considered his words. "Really?"

Dylan nodded. "Really."

"Tomorrow," she said.

He sighed. "Okay, tomorrow, but I'm holding you to it. You're no fun when you're miserable and in love."

The next day when Celeste stopped by the restaurant, it was closed. Following a hunch, she drove out to Tank's diner. She found Jimmy seated at the counter, drinking coffee and trading good-natured insults with Tank. She hesitated when she stepped inside. Tank saw her first and immediately filled a mug with coffee. He gestured to a stool next to Jimmy, who seemed to be the only customer.

"I was wondering when you'd be by again," Tank said.

Jimmy had the grace to look embarrassed. "I'm sorry I called you what I did."

She waved her hands. "I must have played my part pretty well. Don't worry about it."

"No, he needs to apologize," Tank said. "Kid needs to learn you don't insult women."

Celeste felt the stir in the air. She turned and watched Luc walk from the rear of the diner. Her heart sank when she saw his blank expression.

"How is Paulie doing?" he asked.

"He says he wants to be punished," she said, tamping down the hurt she felt at the emotional distance he put between them.

"The attorney I got him said Paulie's pleading guilty. He admitted to everything." Jimmy's face twisted with grief. "If anyone had told me Paulie did those things I would have called them a damn liar. Anyone but him."

"He's facing multiple rape charges and one charge

of murder," she said quietly. "While he didn't deliberately kill her, he did cause her death." She looked directly at Luc, silently pleading with him to return her gaze.

"Jimmy, come on back here and show me how you make those fancy eggs," Tank said suddenly.

Jimmy glanced from Celeste to Luc. "Sure." He slid off the stool and started to walk around the counter. Then he stopped. "Are you really going to let the best thing in your life get away? Hell, Luc, even cops need love." He walked back into the kitchen area with Tank.

"I didn't want it to happen this way," she said miserably.

"I know," Luc said quietly. He took a deep breath. "Jimmy and I have talked about all this. We'll do what we can to help Paulie. We're keeping the restaurant closed for a month or so. Too many people coming in for the thrill, not for the food." He paused. "I just wish I'd realized it sooner. I was driving away and suddenly remembered a time when Paulie said all women deserve love and roses."

"And that's when you knew," she murmured.

He nodded. He lifted his head and stared at her.

"I'm not the easiest person to be with. I figured I would always be alone. Convinced myself I was better off that way. The trouble is, I didn't plan on meeting you and realizing I don't want to be alone anymore. I want you in my life, Celeste." A corner of his mouth lifted. "Even if you're a cop."

Her heart soared at his words. She took one step forward, then another, then ran into his arms.

"Hell, Celeste, your parents are going to tell you you're making the mistake of your life," he told her.

"Are you kidding? They'll be ecstatic I found some-one," she assured him with a lilt in her voice.

He looked down at her upturned face and shook his head. "Lady, you scare the hell out of me, but I love you and want to marry you."

"Wow," she whispered. Smiling through her tears, she reached up and cupped his face with her hands. For the first time, she saw true joy in Luc's eyes and face. She didn't think she could imagine any sight more in-credible than the man she loved more than life itself admitting he loved her and wanted to be with her for the rest of his life. "You actually said the *L* word in the same sentence as the *M* word. Don't worry, Luc, I'm scared, too, but something tells me as long as we're together we can do anything."

* * * * *

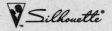

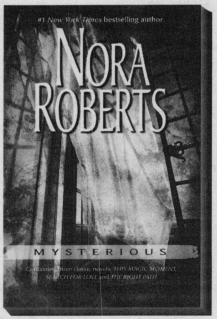